CW00832985

The Keepers

The Keepers

Connor Chronicles Book I

Dormaine G

I dedicate this book to my daddy Charles Richmond, who I miss dearly.

Acknowlegments

I want to say thank you to Kenny, Matt, Sabrina, and Simone. I appreciate you all for your words of encouragement and support, but most of all for pushing me well beyond my limits. Thank you, Megan, Olyvia, Taylen, and Colin Jr. for keeping my inner child alive.

Chapter 1

Where do I begin? I can start by telling you how I am a bubbly, courteous, dependable, straight-A student who has the perfect life. Who wants that? I am ridiculously sarcastic, which for some reason tends to get me into trouble; go figure. I love to sleep a lot, am captain on the swim team, and have two wonderful best friends; and this year my favorite word so far has been "seriously," but recently my life has drastically changed.

I went from a typical teenager, whose biggest concerns were what to wear, taming my obnoxious hair, and avoiding zits, to discovering just how different I was from most people and having to carry that burden of secrecy on my shoulders from the people I most love. I learned the harsh reality that this world is not the safe haven it appears to be and that there are those who help keep such secrets buried. I just became one of them.

Let me back up a few months and start where my life began to unfold, having not a clue on how this day I would come to stand in an old shack deep in the woods, preparing for the fight of my life against the unknown.

First, let me give you some background on my family and myself. I am one of three kids; and yes, as luck would have it, I am smack-dab right in the middle.

There is Ebony, my seventeen-year-old sister who thinks she is perfect in every way. She is the captain of the cheerleading squad, but believe me, it did not go to her head. According to her, she always knew that the "powers that be" made her perfect way before cheer came along. Geez, I just love her to pieces.

She is pretty, petite, and perky, being all of five feet five and a size 2. She has big brown eyes that match her complexion, sexy, full lips, and gorgeously toned legs. At least that is how she describes herself. If you ask me, she reminds me of a horse, a healthy one though, like one of those thoroughbreds. Hey, she has long dark hair that she calls her mane, so it fits.

She is supersmart, as in a genius level, even though you wouldn't know it. I don't get her. She keeps a 3.5 grade average when she could easily have a 4.0. She plays it down to fit in with the cheer team and the jerks, a.k.a. jocks. Don't get me wrong, I don't think cheerleaders are not smart and I'm all for sports, but I swear in my school the cheerleading team is more of a cult. I swear they wear their outfits daily.

All she does is twirl her hair in front of her boyfriend, Robert, and giggle like the rest of the girls on the squad. I asked her once what gives with playing dingy. She told me I wouldn't understand, and maybe when or if a boy would consider me, I might get it. Personally, I thought that was the stupidest answer I had ever heard. Maybe she is not as smart as I thought. As I said, I just don't get it.

At home, she thinks she is second in command to Mom the way she talks to me and tries to give me orders. Sometimes I just want to smack her.

Then there is Kane, my seven-year-old brat of a brother who gets away with murder because he is so adorably cute. *Yeah right!* He does have the cutest smile and the longest eyelashes ever, but that is if you can get past the stench. Half the time, he thinks he's some sort of reptile, and the other half, he smells like one.

He runs around the house and the backyard in a red cape that I am sure can fly on its own by now because it's so dirty. I swear a tornado hits his room every day because it's so messy. There are toys everywhere, and trying to walk in a straight line without stepping on a noise-making gadget is impossible.

He thinks he is this great comedian, but the only joke is he.

He is so funny that the first and last time he sat on my face during my much-needed nap-time, waking me to an aroma of severe toxic fumes, I showed him just how comical he was. I picked him up, laughing the whole way to the hall closet, and threw him in. My memory is hazy, but I think a chair was shoved under the handle so he could not get out, maybe. I'm just saying the memory of the chair incident is vague to me.

Anyway, I forgot to let him out when my ride came to go shopping. Sadly for me, right when we made it to the mall, I got a call from my mom telling me I better get home in twenty minutes or else. That is when I remembered Reptile Boy.

After that, I was out of commission of any kind of social life for two whole weeks.

Then there is me, Sasha. Okay, it is Connor. Yes, I have a boy's name—might as well be. I am fifteen with no prospect of boobs or curves of any kind.

Whom did I piss off?

I'm bony and flat all over, especially in all the wrong places. I am four feet eleven and cannot gain a pound if I tried, and believe me, I have tried. Most girls would say I should be grateful because I don't gain a pound, but I eat and eat and nothing. I outeat most boys, and it's so embarrassing when we go out to dinner. The waiters usually hands my plate to my dad first until I stop them and point to me. As they politely hand the plate over with a smile, they graciously give me a side order of that ever-so-judging look that says, "You will regret it one day." Well, today isn't here, so hand it over.

Lately, I have to eat practically the whole house to maintain my current weight. My mom threatens to take me to the doctor if this keeps up. She said something about me having a tapeworm, so now I resorted to hoarding food in my room for a late-night snack before going to bed so I don't wake up in the middle of the night starving.

My dad, the other comedian in the house, makes comments about having to get a second job to support my food habit. Then of course, Kane has his jokes about putting me out to pasture to let me graze.

My mom cornered me one day after dinner and asked me about smoking those "funny-smelling herbal trees." She actually said that and something about ever needing to talk. I think I stood there with my mouth open until I walked away. Ebony tells me I will never get a boyfriend the way I eat.

You have to love family support.

Then there is my hair. I have big, wild, crazy, curly black hair that half the time I cannot control it, so I stick it in a ponytail with plain elastic; otherwise, it goes every which way.

I'm an undercover science-fiction lover who keeps her collectibles in a wooden mahogany chest at the foot of my bed. The chest was my grandmother's on my mom's side. I begged my mom for it when Nana passed away years back.

My mom thought I wanted it for memory's sake, and though part of that is true, I needed a better place to hide my so-called geeky stuff other than under the closet floorboard in my room. If my dad ever finds out about me pulling up that floorboard, yikes.

As far as school goes, I do well enough whenever I seem to care to try. I constantly have to hear how well Ebony does and that I should try harder like her. Personally, I would rather go play in traffic blindfolded than be like her.

Lastly are the parentals, Mr. Blair and Mrs. Elizabeth Esquibel (Es-skwee-bal). What can I say about them other than they feed us? No, seriously, as far as parents go, they are cool, especially when I hear what my friends go through. My parents are still crazy over each other. They constantly have to touch. It's so gross.

My mom doesn't look her age, so no wrinkles at all, and you cannot get her age out of her either. She said the youthful skin is from the melanin in her skin tone and sunblock. Hey, if I look like her when I am her age, I say bring on the melanin.

She has manageable curly hair that she sticks up all the time and lets loose curls fall where they may. She has no grays yet, but I'm almost positive she has a healthy supply of brown hair dye hidden away in a vault. She is about five feet five with a slim, toned built. What I love most about her is the fact that she loves to laugh at her own corny jokes. Wicked smart too; she has her master's in nursing, so that makes her a nurse practitioner. Years ago, she opened a nonprofit clinic that she absolutely loves. She believes in giving back.

Then there is my dad. He is about six feet and has a slim but muscular build. My parents believe in working out. Dark hair and light brown to hazel eyes that represent his heritage. What can I say about my dad other than he thinks he can perform Jedi mind tricks? Honestly, Dad, grow up already. He does something with computers in corporate America. Both of their jobs sound boring, but hey, they provide me with food, and we all know that is priority.

So bottom line, Ebony took after my mom and Kane my dad in the looks department, so what happened to me? Growing up, I would always ask, "Whom do I look like?" They would always say we come in all different shapes and colors or I look like Aunt So-and-So, but we don't have pictures of everybody in the family. It never really sat well, but I would let it go.

We are one big happy family, well, most of the time. We live in a four-bedroom, two-level, colonial-style house with a nice-sized basement, which is the family room. My dad constantly complains when he has to fix anything in this big old house. According to him, my mom would have never spoken to him ever again if they did not buy this house. It is nice, but it looks like all the other houses in the neighborhood, a dollhouse. It is a white house with a gray door and gray shutters to match. Six tall, narrow shrubs are in the front, which are almost as tall as the house with rosebushes across the front below the windows. A white picket fence runs around to the back where it meets up with a six-foot wooden fence for privacy's sake.

The yard is huge, but my dad refuses to buy a pool. He claims it makes no sense to have a pool year-round when you can only use it three maybe four months out of the year, and we can't afford it.

I don't understand because according to my mom, he made some crazy investment before I was born that set us up for life. Technically, my parents don't have to work, and we still would not go broke. I think he is hiding it in the backyard or something. I'm not bitter or any- thing—okay, maybe just a little bitter—but a pool would be awesome.

The town we live in is uneventful and peaceful. It really doesn't have too much going on other than seasonal town fairs, festivals, and carnivals, a quaint town that fits snuggly in the middle of everything. It is to the right of the big city, left of the water, and almost surrounded by the dreaded woods. Dreaded because I feel someone is always lurking about watching me, like in a scary movie.

My favorite event is our annual summer week-long fishing event. At the end of the week, the town hosts a huge fish fry contest from all the fish caught during the week, and I'm the first in line to try them all. I know this because the peo- ple tell me so, but my shame does not prevent me from stuffing my face. Actually, it got me a spot on the judging panel last year.

The population here is about twenty thousand, so people go to the city if they want some sort of nightlife. I don't know how my parents came to live here, but I actually do love it, and it's home. There is nothing special about the town, except the amazing trick that this town holds is that everyone knows everyone, so trying to get away with anything without getting busted is hard; the chances of getting caught by people who don't know you are virtually impossible.

How great is that?

Even though I love it, it is boring, and there is no privacy. I would love to venture out and explore the rest of the world. Is that not what all young adults want to do?

Oh, by the way, did I mention that I have the ability to become invisible?

No? Guess what, I do.

It's not that I'm such a plain Jane that no one notices me—because people do when they stare at my combative hair or guys come up to me asking about Ebony. I tell them either get lost or she died.

I have the actual no-one-can-see-me invisibility.

The first time I realized it was when we were on a Disney family vacation a few months back. We were at a buffet in Florida, and this cutie started talking to me in line.

He had the nicest eyes. I'm seriously into the shape and color of eyes. He had wavy dark hair and a gorgeous smile, and he was so tall, he towered over me. When he first came up to me, I felt that maybe this punishment of family bonding time might turn out to be fun after all.

Our conversation was going well when out of nowhere, my reptile of a brother decided to give me the wedgie of a lifetime.

I squealed like a pig, grabbed my Wonder Woman boy shorts, tripped into the buffet table, and face-kissed the floor, dragging the tablecloth with me. I tried to catch the food and stop myself from falling, but all I accomplished was taking half the buffet with me and smearing potato salad on my face and clothes. I mean seriously, why me?

As my parents ran over to help, the manager came over, complaining about my behavior and wanting to know who was going to pay for this mess.

It was such a horrible scene. It's hard for me to talk to boys as it is since a lot don't approach me, so I was mortified. My parents were scolding me for my clumsiness while Reptile Boy huddled in the corner laughing. I tried to explain it wasn't me, but they wouldn't even listen. They told me they were going to dock my allowance to compensate them for paying for the mess I made.

I turned around; and my little cutie, who didn't even try to help me, was clear across the room talking to Ebony. She didn't hear a thing or at least pretended not to; either way, they both sucked.

I went back to our room to clean up. I was so upset after what happened but felt worse after I saw what I looked like in the bathroom mirror. I stood there wishing I could just disappear into a black hole.

I hopped into the shower to clean off, and by the time I got out and wiped off the mirror, I couldn't see my reflection. At first, I thought I went blind, but no, because I could see other things, just not me. Then I thought I died of pure humiliation and did a rejoicing jig.

Not that I want to die, but I feel that I have accomplished a lot in my youth, and it was a better option than family bonding time, a.k.a. torture. I started to see my reflection again, and my heart sank so low that I stood there pouting.

Then it hit me—*I was invisible!*

Chapter 2

I go to Randell High, a typical redbrick school housing two stories of adolescent craziness due to uncontrollable hormones. My school houses ninth through twelfth graders.

For a small town, our school consists of a gymnastics team, a swim team, a hockey team, a soccer team, and a basketball team. We also have a step team, ranked number 1 in our division, and of course our all-star football team. I guess the grown folk around here want us teens to stay busy so we don't find trouble.

Like all other schools, freshmen, a.k.a. "cabbage heads," are picked on. I have no clue where that name came from, but it's a tradition. The seniors, mostly jocks, tend to do the torturing; and when I say torture, I mean stuffing the cabbage heads in lockers, dumping them in garbage cans, or locking them into the bathroom storage closets besides whatever else.

Every so often, Mr. Stuckey, the principal, rescues one sad soul encapsulated by metal restriction. As if being rescued by the principal is not humiliating enough, bringing him to class is even worse, which is a major no-no because they, the students rescued, tend to be condemned to a life of never-ending cruelty. One would be better off running away from the principal and getting detention.

Rule is if you cannot wiggle your way out of forced purgatory, then stay there until the bully who put you in gets you out. If you yell for help or whine about it, then it is the same thing as ratting them out. How twisted is that?

On the other hand, the new girls get the threatening stares, the snide looks, and the occasional shove. I obviously signed up for a fashion-slash-popularity contest that I was clearly not aware I entered.

I muddle through without any help from Ebony, who feels I should toughen it out. She holds as much sympathy as what a thimble can hold, an itty-bitty metal one that doesn't give an ounce. I would say she is part vampire since her personality is so draining it sucks the joy right out of my life, but vampires I like—her, not so much. She is definitely part something unnatural. I just haven't figured out what yet.

We only have one person that tends to the unnatural hygienic wonders of this school, and I don't know how he does it. It's remarkably spotless even though he is hardly around. His name is Mr. Johnston, but we call him Ole Man Johnston since he moves like an old man.

He appears to be in his mid-thirties, is muscular, and has a perfectly round shiny bald head. He never smiles, ever, as if he carries the weight of the world on his shoulders from an unfortunate past. One would think he was healthy enough to work anywhere. I think it has something to do with a type of certain liquid refreshment that is illegal for a young person like me. If you speak, he will respond, but that's as far as the conversation ever goes because he always strolls off after that.

I heard he was in a bad car accident years ago that made him crazy, that's why he stays to himself mostly, and that he lives in the school basement. I don't believe it, the basement part, but I don't have any plans of finding out.

I have too many other things going on in my life to concern myself with, like my studies, or the lack of in my case. My parents impressed upon me if I didn't bring up my grades, I will be sentenced to my bedroom for all eternity. Eternity was only until the end of school year, but that is excessively long, it might as well be the end of my life.

So I devised a plan to avoid my tests to give myself more time to study. Therefore, every time there was one, I would go invisible, or rather, using my preferred terms, "unseen," "disappear," or "vanish." Only my plan wretchedly fails every time. I tried and tried for months with no such luck. It was as if "the powers that be" were sitting around conspiring against me. I started to think it was all in my head and that I'm officially certifiable.

Seriously, I should be upset at the fact that it even happened or at least shocked, but no, I was excited about it. For once, I felt special; you know, different.

Then it finally did happen again when I slipped right in front of Robert, Ebony's boyfriend, the hottest boy in school. He is six feet two, captain of the football team, and smells oh so heavenly.

Angela and I were walking in the hall between classes after they must have attempted to clean up a spill.

Angela, who is my age and one of my best friends, is sweet but unscrupulously nosy. When she knows something is up, she will figure it out, trust me. She is maybe four inches taller than I am and wears only the trendiest fashions from off the runways. Just between you and me, her mom sews her fabulous clothes, but you can't tell. Her mom happens to be a tailor who can make anything from Italian-style wedding dresses to edgy rocker wear.

Anyway, I didn't notice the bright yellow Wet Floor sign right in front of me. It should have been a big fat yellow sign that read "Hey, idiot, watch out, you're about to bite it for the hundredth time." That I would have seen.

One minute I was standing upright talking to Angela, the next I was spread-eagled in front of the kid and his teammates with my skirt up. There was a crowd around me to watch the show, staring, this time, at my Superman boy shorts and me. People were laughing, pointing, and cheering at my not-so-graceful landing. Someone yelled, "Hey, Superman, she's calling you!" or "Why are you wearing your brother's underwear?"

I was wet and embarrassed. I really should not get emotional about these situations anymore, honestly. My sister was right there glaring at me. As if I did it on purpose.

She bent over, and I thought she'd help me up, but no. Instead she whispered, "Stop humiliating me" in my ear. She at least pulled down my skirt before she stood up and walked off with Robert consoling her.

Seriously!

Angela came over to help me up. I thanked her and ran to the bathroom. She yelled for me to wait up as she gathered my books. No way. I was out. I ran warp speed, knowing she could never catch up with me.

I made it to the bathroom hardly anyone used. It's supposed to be haunted according to, well, everybody. I think Ole Man Johnston made it up so he can get his drink on.

Once again, I stood in front of the mirror totally humiliated. I was wiping my boy shorts off with a paper towel, thinking how I wanted to die. The Superman comments were unnecessary.

After I finished drying myself off with the bathroom hand dryer, I rechecked myself in the mirror, but my reflection wasn't there. I couldn't believe it—my reflection was gone, even my clothes, yet I could see my hands, arms, legs, everything when I looked down.

It did happen. I didn't imagine it; it actually happened. At least I think so, unless crazy runs in my family. Only one way to find out if it's true is to put it to the test, right? There are people out in the hallway, which makes it the perfect opportunity, so here goes nothing.

I headed toward the front hallway's main entrance, not sure why that direction, but that was where I decided to go. It was about fifty feet to the door, and it was in between classes, so that meant a crowd of teens in my way doing nothing. I held my breath passing people all while thinking to myself, "Please don't change back, please don't change back."

I passed the front office where Mrs. Potts, the office administrator, sat, staring off in my direction, but she didn't say anything to me. Even if she could see me, she probably wouldn't notice me; she's always on the phone, not working. Everyone knows the only reason she got the job is because she's the principal's niece.

I constantly glanced around, making sure I didn't run into anybody. I evaded a couple not paying attention to anyone else except each other, dodging a flying hand from a girl describing something large, and avoided getting slapped by a swinging backpack. It was like playing dodge ball, but for once during break, I succeeded in not getting hit.

I spotted my sister by her locker and was almost tempted to trip her so she knew how it felt to be embarrassed but decided against it. With my luck, I would enjoy it too much and get busted. Not knowing how this works, I kept on my mission ahead: my freedom.

Finally, I made it to the front entrance without anyone detecting me.

I made it outside as soon as the second bell rang, which meant you should be in your next class seated, according to school law. As expected, no one was or supposed to be outside. It was midmorning, and a cool misty rain greeted me outside, which made the perfect weather to snuggle up somewhere warm. No one will be home until much later, so I decided to head that way for a much-needed snack nap. A snack nap is when you eat a lot of snacks until your belly is full then take a nap.

If the principal decided to call my parents, I will tell them something about not signing in, then throw in the nurse's office to mix things up a bit. Lame, I know, but I kind of didn't plan this jailbreak.

The more I thought about it, the realization of unpreparedness dawned on me. For example, my plan would include a raincoat that hung in my locker; if only I waited until the coast was clear and grabbed what I needed. Too late now. This is what I get for trying to fly by the seat of my pants.

After making it to the last tree in front of the school, I allowed myself a whopping deep breath.

"Psst."

Whipping my head around to see what was up, I nearly jumped when this kid caught my attention. He was standing behind a huge oak tree, waving me over. I must have tunnel vision because I didn't even notice him standing there.

When did I become visible again? How does this thing work? I told myself to stay calm. Obviously, he goes here too, so chances are he is skipping too.

I cautiously complied as he stood there waiting for me. He didn't look familiar; I had never seen him around before today. He wore loose dark jeans and a red T-shirt with an unfamiliar logo and had about seven inches on me. He leaned against the tree with his arms folded.

He asked, "Where are you headed in such a hurry?" At first, I didn't know what to say. He never talked to me before, so why now? Plus, why would he call me out and make himself known? I was completely caught off guard and stumped. "You can see me? I mean, I'm sick, so I'm headed home." If this was football, that, ladies and gentlemen, would be called a fumble.

He raised his left eyebrow, giving me the once-over, and said, "You don't look sick to me. What's your name by the way?" I overlooked his eye tour and was hesitant to respond due to nerves but decided to play along. What is the worst that can happen? I will probably never speak to this kid again. "Connor."

"Antony, but people call me Tony for short," he said. Don't recall asking but didn't want to sound rude, so instead I asked, "Why are we having small talk on the school lawn right now when we need to jet before we're caught?"

As soon as I asked the question, my neighbor, Mrs. Palmer, came jogging over. "Connor, Connor, is that you?" My mouth fell open as she called me out. Busted. Why

did she need to walk by at this precise moment?

That was Tony's cue to take off, but before he was out of hearing range, he asked, "It's cool, huh?"

I thought that was a strange thing to say, but there were more important matters to concern myself with now, like Mrs. Palmer breathing on the back of my neck making my skin crawl. I slowly turned to face her standing there not three inches from me.

"Why are you out of school?" she asked.

Seriously, she is always around at the worst times. Is Nosy Nelly the new Secret Service? Because obviously I must be important.

"Connor, are you listening to me? I hope you are not skipping. I must call your mother right now. She is on the PTA, and this does not make her look good at all." She asked but didn't wait for a response before fumbling in her fanny pouch. Sure enough, she called my mom right in front of me.

I slumped back against the tree and sighed. I'm in so much trouble.

That evening at home, I got the scolding of a lifetime. I think I aged about ten years standing there, trying to act as if I was listening. The whole time, Reptile Boy was in the hallway on the floor, laughing and pointing at me through the cracked doorway, but I didn't even care.

I tend to fade out when I'm being mentally abused by my parents; I have mastered the art of nodding and saying "uh-huh, uh-huh, uh-huh." I caught phrases like "We try our best" and "Not acting like an adult," which I thought was a silly thing to say. If I were an adult, would I still live here? No way.

I quoted my usual lines: "Yes, Mom," "No, Dad," "I don't know what I was thinking," and "Promise, I won't do it again." My dad looked at me sadly, as if he was so disappointed that his little girl would ever skip school. Then the comedian came out of him and mumbled something to my mom about the possibility of me taking drugs. My mom swatted him, then he tickled her. They are so disgustingly gross.

The wardens pardoned me, but if it happened again, I will be sentenced for a month to a life of boredom. That meant no phone, no computers, no TV, no friends, no life. They might as well send me to a Nunnery and be done with it.

Later that night, I was lying in my room thinking of the kid Tony who I bumped into outside after my little taste of freedom. Why did he say "It's cool?" When did I become visible again? Also, why am I not freaked out about what occurred today?

Probably because it's cool. I mean, who doesn't want superpowers? Okay, maybe that is a stretch, but honestly, I like it.

Not able to concentrate on my homework, I decided to go to bed early. I drifted off to sleep thinking about the endless possibilities of invisibility.

Chapter 3

I woke up to the rousing of the wind whistling. It sounded like a storm was brewing and was about to land at any minute. I covered my head with my cozy down blanket and rolled over drifting back to sleepville.

I stirred for the second time tonight from a commotion at my window. It was a repetitious clatter, preventing me from going back to sleep, probably the tree branches taking a beating from the stormy wind knocking into my window.

Worried about rain getting in, I unburied myself from my safe haven and checked to see what time it was. My alarm clocked glowed 2:00 a.m., still early enough for me to get a few more hours of sleep.

I rolled out of bed to make sure both sides of my windows were closed, since I have a habit of forgetting to latch them before going to bed. There was a chill in the air, forcing me to slip on my bunny slippers, Mr. Ears, to keep my toes warm. I stumbled over, and to no surprise, they were slightly open.

I loved when it rained, and watching it was one of my favorite things to do. I guess that is why I love swimming so much, simply because I love the water. I peered out only to find a clear sky.

As I stared out, I heard my name below. I looked down and saw Tony standing in the bushes, holding some pebbles. He was the noise I kept hearing, not the trees or wind against my windowpane. He motioned for me to come down and pointed toward my backyard.

"What are you doing here? You better leave before someone sees you," I tried to whisper, but it didn't quite come out that way. I am going to be grounded if my dad hears this.

"I'm not leaving until you come down," he whispered. "Fine." Not that I am easy or anything. I mean, I just met the boy, but curiosity caught the better of me, so I decided to go. "Give me two minutes," I said and held up
two fingers.

"Hurry," he whispered.

Who does he think he is, my dad?

I shut the window and locked it, then remembered locking it before going to bed earlier. I remember because my dad said it might rain tonight so I should make sure it's closed. Maybe something is wrong with the latch. I will have my dad check it later today.

After popping a piece of gum into my mouth, I snuck down, making sure I didn't step on the side of the steps that creaked. I perfected this technique a long time ago when I used to sneak downstairs after my bedtime to play video games in the basement. Zombies everywhere beware.

As far as basements go, ours didn't have that huge scary cast-iron boiler, so it was safe. As irrational as that sounds, those old boilers look as if they want to gobble up little kids.

Keeping the light off, I kept checking my surroundings to make sure my mom was not waiting for me around the corner. Sometimes she stays up late to watch old black-and-white movies.

The coast was clear, and the back door was guard free. I turned off the motion-sensor light to outside before going out, not wanting to awaken the next-door neighbors.

The full moon should provide enough lighting for us to see. Since it's a full moon, I hope Ebony is not out about in her true form attacking people.

As soon as I closed the back door, I saw him waiting on the far side of the patio, trying to play it cool, watching me walk over. I could clearly see him sitting on the ledge of the patio with a hood draped partly over his head, facing me. It was cooler out than I thought.

I was rubbing the goose bumps on my arms and asked, "What's up?" What was so important that it could not wait until tomorrow at school? I wondered.

He pulled off his hooded sweatshirt and handed it to me. I couldn't help but smile. I thanked him and hurriedly put it on. He stood there with his hands in his pockets as I fumbled with it, since it was huge and I was not. After I remembered how to dress myself, he asked, "Can you meet us at the school Friday night around midnight?"

I didn't notice before, but he was kind of cute. No, I take that back—he was really cute.

"Hello, Earth to Connor," he asked, waving a hand in front of me to get my attention.

"Yes? Why me, and who are 'we'? How do you know where I live? Are you stalking me?" I asked all at once. Who am I kidding? This is such a small town, everyone knows someone.

He smiled and shook his head, suppressing a laugh. "I'm not stalking you, relax. I know you have like a thousand questions, but trust me, we will answer them the best we can on Friday," Tony said.

"What are you talking about?" It was hard to register what he was saying. I was still half asleep.

He cocked his head and looked at me funny. "Umm, because you have the ability to not be seen," he answered.

Woooow, that was an eye-opener. I so did not see that coming. I stood there dazed and confused.

"Hello, invisible, undetected, whatever word you want to use," he added, stressing the point even further.

"How do you know?" I asked.

"I know this sounds crazy, but I am able to see you. Remember, I called you out today?" he said.

"Yes, I remember but…"

"What, did you think you were the only one?" he asked, cutting me off. "That's strange because I was drawn to the others."

"There are others? How many others?" I asked.

"You definitely need to come Friday night so we can all meet. Weird, I thought you sensed me yesterday that's why you came out front," he said.

"No, I didn't have a clue. I thought it was just me," I said.

"That would be a no," he said.

"Well, I did. I am not trying to sound obnoxious or anything, but I really had no clue. I don't know about this school midnight meeting."

He smirked at me. "Your choice," he said, then he took off, hopping the fence in one swift movement, and just like that, he was gone, not even so much as a good-bye. I was starting to think that was his MO.

Did he really just jump a six-foot fence? I was about to yell "Wait," remembering I still had his hood on, but it was too late. He was gone. I stood outside on the patio for a while, letting everything he said soak in. I'm not the only one. I'm not sure how I felt about that.

Sneaking back upstairs, I made it back to my room and pulled off his hood. His cologne smelled nice. When I passed my bedroom mirror, I was horrified with what I was wearing. First time a boy visits me at my window, I wear not only pajamas with a hole in the neck, but my sci-fi Stargate SG1, the one Angie's mom sewed for me. That is why he was staring at me when I came out. He wasn't playing it cool; he was in shock.

Connor, you are so sexy.

Chapter 4

The next day before first period started, I was fumbling through my locker, rummaging for nothing in particular, trying not to make eye contact with Angela as she drilled me for information like the fanatical person she can be.

When she gets like this, she talks a mile a minute; her voice goes up to just under a squeal. If she doesn't know what is going on, all is wrong with her world, and she will not let up until she pries every bit of information out of you. I most definitely see news reporter in her future.

"What happened? Where did you go yesterday? You didn't come back to class. I had to call your house last night, since you didn't pick up your cell...," she said, staring me down.

I knew her well enough to know she was frustrated not knowing why I left, since tripping is common for me, and upset because I would not confide in her. "And your brother said you could not come to the phone, something about you being on a leash out back, so I hung up on him.

You could have called. I was worried, you know." She finished by slamming a book back into her locker next to mine.

That is so true, she worries so much. Ever since her adopted brother Vincent went missing twelve years ago, she has a habit of getting frantic when not warranted.

He was a year older than she was, and they were close. He was her big brother. His father died when he was a baby, and unfortunately, his mother was not in the picture. With no other family to go to, he ended up a ward of the state and went to an orphanage. Eventually, Angela's parents took him in right before she was born.

I was three when it happened, but I do have some memories of him since we played together. It was my first exposure to sadness how could it not stick in your head.

Angela cried so much back then, and her family took it hard. She stayed with me a lot, and that seemed to have helped us both. My parents said the police and community were involved in the search. Even Mr. Bucks, a.k.a. the boss, my dad would call him, backed the search for him for weeks, but he was never found.

My parents were overprotective of me for years after that, eventually easing up when I started protesting. Ever since then, I try to be a little understanding when Angela gets like this because she means well.

Putting my left hand halfway up, surrendering, cutting her off, and allowing her to catch her breath, I explained, "Sorry, but I was put into a boredom coma from the parentals, lecturing me on the responsibility of young adulthood and leaving school without permission and how it was not a smart thing to do."

She waited for more information, clutching her books for dear life, but what do I say? I ran into the bathroom from pure humiliation, disappeared, literally, then ran out to find another kid who could possibly do the same thing. I don't think so.

I felt bad I couldn't tell her, but I have no desire to go to the funny farm. I heard most of them don't bathe, and that is nasty. I made up some barely believable story of running out due to dirty wet clothes.

Besides, I do not want to give her more to worry about. I don't think she ate it, but she let it go when she realized I wasn't going to elaborate. That or the first bell stopped her next question.

As I walked off, I could feel her eyes digging into me and hear the wheels turning in that brain of hers, and that was not good.

I sat next to Hope in math class in first period like usual. Hope was my other best friend my age. She is cute as a button, with the biggest darkest eyes, soft, shiny, bouncy reddish-brown hair, and about Angie's height. She is what her family calls Creole and has exactly five freckles on her nose. Her family comes from New Orleans, so she grew up speaking fluent French, or a version of it. She is the nicest person you would ever want to meet. She is incredibly passive to the point where she makes it easy for people pick on her. That is where Angie and I come in.

Five years ago, we stepped in when some girls were harassing her because her family doesn't have a lot of money. They were teasing her about her clothes and the fact that she lived on the outskirts of town. Now we're known as the *tres amigas*, well, to us anyway. That and with the help of Angela's mom, who sews her clothes to help financially, she had more confidence. She discovered her own style, hippie bohemian, but she can rock some cool jeans too. Her boyfriend situation is another story.

I was jolted back to present day when I heard her say something about me glowing, so it must be a boy. "Whatever," I said, and added most of the boys from this school are way too immature for me. My goal is to go to school in Paris and do as the French do. She agreed, and we laughed at each other.

I didn't mention that after Paris, I would somehow become a part of a secret space organization and fly my own spaceship that they will name after me one day. I felt the need to leave that part out and to keep that to myself.

Our teacher purposely put a halt to our good mood by handing out a pop quiz. Great.

After fourth period ended, Hope spotted some strange boy behind us as we headed to the grand cafe, a.k.a. the lunchroom. "I think he has been following us since last class," she said, not being slick about it at all by literally pointing him out.

Grabbing her hand and pushing it down, I turned around and saw a kid I have never seen before. His hair was greasy, and he wore all black with holes in his pants, the kind of holes that were not on purpose but from wear and tear. He was staring right at me, and from the expression on his face, he didn't seem thrilled to see me, but I didn't know him. I don't know why, but I had a funny feeling about him.

Hope covered her mouth with her book, laughing at me. "Is that your new boyfriend, Connor?"

"What new boyfriend, and why didn't I hear about this sooner?" Angela asked, coming up from behind. Hope filled her in, all while giggling at my expense. Great, something else Angela will grill me on.

"Um, he is gross, and I don't have a boyfriend." We made it to the lunchroom finally, and I was grateful for the noise distraction since they found it necessary to hound me about him all the way here.

Lunch was the same as always; the jocks sat with the evil cheerleaders. My sis is dead center, sitting next to her boyfriend Robert. I would never admit to her how hot he is.

After school, he works at his dad's law firm to prep him for the bar when he graduates law school. I hate to break it to his dad, but Robert is not "the brightest bulb in the pack."

He has always needed a tutor, and that's how Ebony and Robert met. She started tutoring him in seventh grade on three classes, hence her popularity and not since birth, as she would have you believe. She was actually human before cheer and didn't care so much about how she looked or if she fit in with the "in crowd."

He does seem to care for my sister, I have to admit, and her for him. They are always together and seem to have fun. Hey, it is a cohesive relationship. Whatever works, right?

Robert's family worships the ground Ebony walks on because she has taken him far, and they know it. All I am saying is his dad needs to lower his educational expectations.

Walking by the jock table, she gave me the stink eye when I attempted to wave, so I politely made her "read between the lines." I swear my mom drank blood when she was pregnant with her. I am just waiting on the devil to come claim his evil spawn when the time is right.

Passing the table, someone yelled, "Help, Superman," and I swore Ebony punched him, but I pretended I didn't see it and kept walking.

Then there are the nerds/geeks, which covers chess, the science club, math club, and LARP (live action role-play). Even though I love science fiction, I wouldn't dress up and run around in a costume, just pajamas in the middle of the night, oh and Halloween, my most favorite holiday.

Some of them are actually cool, like Angela's boyfriend, Bobby, and yes, that is his real name, not Robert, who doesn't dress up, but there is the other half who knows how smart they are and turn their nose up at you.

Barnabus, the freckled redheaded kid who wants to take over the world, is the rudest individual that roams the earth. He feels the need to tell you just how inferior you are to him. Just about after every math and science class, he gets beat up or locker bound because he expresses his annoyance of us mere humans' retarded intelligence, and yet he runs around in costumes playing live games. Some nerve.

The Victims of Eternal Richness dress in black, brand name only, and act like their lives are so hard because their parents are so disgustingly filthy rich, they must suffer for it. Give me a break.

The ringleader we call Cricket because she chirp-chips all the time about nothing and does the most complaining. They either sleep around or threaten suicide, which no one has attempted that I know of, and thank goodness for that. The problem, as I see it, is that their parents are out making so much money, they feel neglected at home, so they come to school craving attention. See, I pay attention in psychology. I say quit complaining and tell it to a therapist one day like the rest of us.

The Individuals sit outside; this includes the skateboarders, extremist, artists, and musicians. No one really pays them too much attention because they'd rather do their own thing. They sit around playing guitar with wool hats on, even in warm weather, while performing some death-defying stunt. I have to admit they are good. It is as if they have no fear.

There is this kid named Bradley but whom we call Cannon because he is so fast on the long board. It is as if he is shoots right out of one.

I peered out the window to watch and, for the first time, noticed Tony. He was doing a long board stunt right off the side railing. Wow, he was good. His nicely sculpted muscles were showing under his muscle shirt. I was staring so hard, I hadn't realized he was staring back at me. I released my bag from my death grip, nodded at him with a half grin, and walked off to catch up with the others.

I glanced back to find him still staring at me while tossing his board in the air. I hurriedly turned away and cut the line for lunch. I got a couple of catcalls but didn't care until someone said, "Let Superman through, she needs fuel for her next save." Will I ever live that down?

I sat with my usual crew, the "Can't wait to get out of this town" group. My group consisted of about eight of us who discussed plans for the future, like where we would live and what we would do. As we were making plans for the near future like this weekend, I thought about Tony's invite this Friday night. I told them I have a family obligation that I couldn't ditch. They accepted it and quickly changed the subject.

Chapter 5

Friday finally came, and I couldn't be more anxious or obnoxious. Concentrating in school was not an option at all, so breezing by today was my game plan. Unfortunately for me, all of my teachers must have known about my well-laid plan and banded together to abolish it.

Each one of them called on me for answers to questions that I had not heard them ask in the first place. I had to keep asking them to repeat themselves, and like the last teacher before them, the repeated question came with a stern look. It was cruel and torturous.

My friends kept asking me all day what was wrong. I just blew them off and told them I must be getting sick or something. I even coughed a couple of times for sympathy's sake, no-go. Angela kept eyeing me because my behavior was off. Okay, so I seriously need to work on my acting skills. Got it.

Later on at home, everyone, except Miss Cheer Cult Queen Ebony, was in the den when my parents asked me if everything was okay since I didn't have plans to go out.

I told them that it is not as if going out is that important. "There are times I like being close to home," I added, hoping they would appreciate that last bit.

That too was a no-go, so after a dramatic pause filled with blank stares and chirping crickets, I told them my plans were actually tentative. My parents gave each other a look, then looked back at me. My mom felt the need to give me a hug; for what, I do not know. Maybe it's a mom thing.

Kane chimed in as usual and added, "Oh, I know. It's a full moon tonight, so she has to lock herself up in the basement before she turns all hairy and monster like." At least he called me a she and not an it.

He really needs to stop watching my scary movie collection. Actually, that is my fault. I used to make him watch them with me when I babysat him.

I told them a nap sounds good right about now. Not really, but I wanted to break out and get away from the "I have two heads" stares. Is it so strange that a teenager wants to stay home on a Friday night to be with her parents and younger brother? Who am I kidding? Yes, it is.

In my room, I must have watched the clock a thousand times, debating going or not. All day, even in school, I kept coming up with excuses not to go. So far, I came up with "maybe this occurred because I was in some freak accident my parents never told me about" or "my mom had to have taken some drugs when she was pregnant with me."

My mind was in a world of its own wondering about what-ifs. I couldn't stop myself. I concluded that I was crazy and hallucinated all of this. That had to be it, right?

If that is the case, I definitely didn't want to go. I will just stay here and vegetate. I will tell Tony I don't want to get involved, if there even is a Tony. Let's face it, I have only spoken to him when no one else was around, and why was this week the first time I noticed him at school? I'm telling you, I'm nuts, as I sit here talking to myself. Ugh!

A nap was attempted but failed, so I lay across my bed, staring up at the ceiling. Some time had passed, and it was dark out because the stars on my ceiling were glowing along with my glow-in-the-dark spaceship. I was still anxious and unable to focus on anything else, now frustrated because I couldn't think of anything else.

That was it. I needed to know what was going on with me or if I was just plain crazy. I wondered if there were some other kids at school involved. Well, I guess there is only one way to find out. I jumped up, changed into comfortable clothing, and off I went.

Checking the clock that said eleven thirty, I hurried up. My parents were in bed by now, and Reptile Boy was fast asleep. Ebony had come in earlier just long enough to change and head back out for her date. I can expect her to sneak in later.

I told my parents that I decided to go out after all and that Angela would be picking me up. I will wait outside for her, so she won't have to ring the bell, waking Kane up.

Half dazed, my mom said okay, not realizing how late it is. They don't like me leaving the house after ten o'clock at night for whatever reason. I can be out past ten, but they feel anything worth doing should start before then.

I quietly walked down the stairs, not wanting to wake my mom up so she could think to ask any questions. As soon as I shut the door, I set off down the block. I only have a permit, so I couldn't ask to borrow the car yet. It was about a twenty-minute walk, so I hurried along to get there on time.

We live in a safe town, so I can walk without worrying about some creepy person in a mask coming after me. Then again, I am surprisingly strong for a girl; as my dad always used to say, I'm manly strong. How unflattering is that?

The one time Ebony and I fought was the last. It was a year ago, over something stupid. I was tired of her telling me what to do, so I pushed her when she got in my face. That turned into a push fest until I flung her into the laundry room pantry from the hallway. I don't even know how I did it.

To hear her tell it, I picked her up over my head like some She-Ra, swung her around several times, and hurled her twenty feet, then stood over her growling. She screamed like a wild animal, acting as if someone was murdering her.

I never told anyone, but I even scared myself a little.

My dad could not stop laughing after Mom checked on Ebony, who was fine but needed to play it up. He teased me about it and told me I should take up cage fighting. On the other hand, my mom was not too happy with me and had me tested for drugs; she seriously did.

I chucked it up saying my adrenaline kicked in after years of pent-up frustration, and that is what the doctor said when the test results came back clean. So see, I can take care of myself.

Tonight, like any other night, it was typically peaceful other than a dog barking at who knows what and the trees rustling from the wind. The temperature was perfect, and the breeze felt nice across my face. It must have been in the sixties tonight, so my zip up was perfect.

I could smell the water from my house, so the tide was high. The air outside smelled like a strange combination of salty seaweed and damp earth blowing over from the ocean. I love the smell of the ocean. I don't know why people complain about it. Wherever I move, it has to be by water.

I heard an unfamiliar sound so I stopped walking. Not anything alarming, but it alerted me to how quiet it had become. Dogs were no longer barking, and the wind no longer blew, how strange. I stood still for a moment waiting for it, then the noise stirred again, and even though it wasn't an alarming sound, I couldn't place what it was. The hairs on my neck stood straight up, and my ears were ringing from the silence.

I sensed someone close, so my eyes scanned the area, searching for movement, but saw nothing. How typical, a girl walks alone at night, hears footsteps, then goes missing. Maybe I need to stop watching scary movies too. Nah. I stayed there for a minute longer listening, just to be sure, then shook it off.

The dogs started up again, and who can stop the wind? I'm losing it—it's got to be my nerves acting up over tonight. I walked on, stargazing. The stars were out shining bright, smiling down on me. Oh, how I wish to be up there one day in my spaceship called the *Connor*. I laughed at myself, as my mind wondered about the adventures I would have. I'm going to pretend I didn't just think that.

I made it to the school in record time but realized I had no clue where we were going to meet. "No spaceship pajamas tonight," I heard Tony say, approaching from behind me out of nowhere.

I spun around. "Ha-ha, funny, and they were Star...

I mean, those weren't mine," I lied.

"Are you sure? Because they sure seemed like your size," he asked with a smile the size of Texas on his face. He had on baggy jeans, a plain black shirt that hugged his chest just right, and the latest pair of footwear. He looked nice.

I had to laugh. "Anyway, why do you keep popping up? Were you following me tonight?" I asked.

"Don't you wish? I was headed this way too. Remember, I invited you? I forgot to tell you where we were meeting. Besides it's difficult to get to, so I would have to take you anyway. Glad you thought long and hard about it and came," he said with a smirk on his face. I told him just what he could do with that smirk. He laughed and said, "This way please." He was holding out his arm with his hands tucked in his jeans pockets, so I obliged.

We headed toward the back of the school, past the football field and the outside basketball court while trying to follow along the track. We were trying to avoid the wet grass as long as possible. I don't recall it raining earlier, so I'm guessing it was wet from the sprinklers.

It was a little eerie late at night with just the two of us, being so used to this placed filled with people talking, laughing and bells that could wake the dead. We barely spoke as we hurried along; it was already midnight.

We headed toward a part of the school that was not attached to the main building. It sat tucked away in the back, so I had never really paid it much attention. They, meaning Mr. Johnston, warned us students to stay away since it contained dangerous machinery, so I did. Especially knowing how clumsy I am and having gotten used to all my limbs, I would like them to stay just where they are, thank you very much.

Tony, now directly in front of me, was leading the way. There were no more tracks to use, so we cut across the grass, dodging any lights, just in case anyone was around. Reaching the building, it was maybe fifty feet wide and appeared to be made of metal. It looked old, a little rusty, and practically surrounded by vines with little red flowers on them that smelled sweet.

In front of the door, Tony handed me a flashlight and told me to turn it on. His was in hand, ready to go. The door creaked a little upon opening but didn't provide any resistance.

Once inside, I looked around, only to be a little disappointed to discover it was just the boiler room, not heavy machinery or something a little more exciting. I figured we would find a workshop for Santa's elves or something like that since the threat of expulsion hung over our heads if caught in here.

"Mr. Johnston never remembers to lock the door, but just to play it safe, I leave a piece of tape over the lock," Tony said, pointing to the tape over the latch. "I replace it every time we have a meeting to make sure we will be able to get in."

Half listening to him, I scanned the room with my flashlight as Tony closed the door. It was bigger inside than I expected. The vines covered a lot. There was plywood and other green machines inside, nothing interesting at all.

I just nodded as reality set in. I couldn't believe I'm doing this. My bravado was starting to fade quickly. We didn't make a sound inside crossing to the other side of the room except when I squealed like a little girl as a mouse ran past my foot.

He glanced over at me.

I cut him a look as if to say, "Sorry, but they are nasty and carry germs."

We stopped at a bright orange door with a chain and padlock on it. He pulled out a key chain with some keys on it, of course, unlocked the padlock and removed the chain, then unlocked the orange door. He tapped on the door 2-3- 2 like some secret knock, then opened it up. He explained, "That is our code, so when they hear someone coming, they know it is one of us. Don't ask how I got these keys. Trust me, you don't want to know."

Who is this kid sticky fingers Houdini? I was concerned yet excited at that same time, but all I said was "Good idea," in regards to the knock.

We walked down the longest flight of stairs ever. Okay, maybe it was about ten steps, but the hairs on the back of my neck were on end again. Once we reached the bottom step, I said, "I'm stopping right here." This was starting to freak me out.

"You've come too far to stop now. Just a little ways more, it's okay, Sci-fi, no one is going to hurt you," he said, puzzled.

"That's not my name, and I'm not scared, just using a little common sense," I said, standing there with my arms folded. I wanted to tuck tail and run right out of there. That may make me a coward, but at least I will be a live coward. I should have thought this through. I may be walking to my death.

He grabbed my arms while they were still folded and said, "Don't take this the wrong way, but if you used any common sense, then you wouldn't have met a guy you hardly knew, here, at midnight, and followed him this far. I think curiosity had more of a role to play."

"You may be right, but Mr. Common Sense just came knocking. Where are we going?" I pulled back from him, getting the chills not from any draft, but from sheer nerves.

"Just bear with me a little longer. I promise there is nothing to fear. Most of your questions will be answered soon enough, please," he said, almost begging me. His eyes were pleading with me as he extended his hand.

Listening to my gut, which said go, and ignoring my head, which said no, I reluctantly took his hand.

He took a deep long breath of relief and said, "You won't regret this. I promise."

I thought, *Connor, if you get yourself killed, you're going be in serious trouble*; It was something my mom would say ever since I was young. It never made any sense, but I guess it's a mom thing.

After the stairs, we turned left and walked down this dim tunnel lit by wall-mounted candles. The ground and walls looked like they were made of tightly packed mud and some other ingredients to hold it together. It smelled earthy down here. There is just no other way to describe it. It was not unbearable, but apparent.

I had always heard there were tunnels down here, but like most schools, you think they are all tales. Supposedly, it was an underground hide-out for slaves to remain until it was safe for them to travel again. Go figure. You do learn a thing or two in school when you listen.

I asked him, "How do you know about this place or find it?"

"After meeting the others and needing a place to go where we could be safe to practice and not be heard, I remembered from history class that there were supposedly tunnels under our school. I know the teachers told us they were sealed, but I thought, why not check into it anyway. I went down to city hall and did my investigation, only to find out there were plans years ago to seal the tunnels, but it was stopped when this property was bought for the building of our school. They also had the blueprints of the grounds and the tunnels."

"I am amazed and impressed. A man who knows how to get the job done," I said, feeling a little better.

He stopped walking, smiled back at me rubbing his chest, and said, "Well, I try."

I pretended to hurl.

After walking maybe a hundred feet, we stopped at a large room to the right even though the tunnel continued forward. As interested as I was to know how far the tunnel went or where it took you, I was more interested in the here and now. There were three others standing in the middle of the room waiting for us, but no one from my school.

"Welcome to the cave," Tony said as we entered.

The room was decorated with old pictures on the walls, burgundy drapes draped over no windows that I could see, two burgundy leather couches, three black leather chairs, and a cherry-wood coffee table. The room was lit with candles and old cast-iron lanterns, lighting the room quite nicely. It was definitely a female's touch.

"Hello, everybody, this is Connor. Connor, this is Cheyenne, Willow, and Byron." He pointed to each of them as he called their names.

They all said hello in unison.

Willow actually gave me a hug and smiled from ear to ear. She was a cute brunette, wearing curls down to her shoulders, and had big brown eyes. She was endowed in the chest department and had an inch or two over me. She wore a fuzzy pink sweater, a knee-length plain black skirt, light pink-colored tights, and black three-inch-heeled Mary Janes. Not my style, but it seems to suit her. She looked so bubbly sweet standing there, grinning as if I was her new puppy. I bet you could probably catch a cavity just by hanging out with her.

Cheyenne, on the other hand, stood there, observing me with indifference, gave me the once-over in slow motion. She was a tall, leggy girl with shiny, straight jet-black hair to her waist. She was gorgeous, and her brown almond-shaped eyes were distinctive. She wore dark jeans that fit her to a tee (how is that possible), a black tight-fitting sweater, and black boots. Her clothes fit her so perfectly, you would think they were painted on her. She must not have any girlfriends who would trust her around their man.

Byron shrugged and said hello, standing next to Willow with his hands tucked in his pants pockets. He had a low buzz cut and a nice smile. He was the handsome type, tall, maybe five ten, with broad shoulders. He wore khakis with black suspenders over a plaid shirt. His shoes were the preppy type and, I am sure, expensive like all of their outfits.

They looked like models right out of a magazine called *Perfect Preppy USA*, if there was one. I, on the other hand, had on my favorite tattered jeans, some geeky shirt, and my zip up that I now refuse to take off. They didn't look real with their perfect hair, makeup, and let's not ignore their expensive shiny accessories.

Tony said, "So she is the one I have been telling you all about. Connor."

Chapter 6

"Hello," I said with uncertainty. All I could do was stand there on display.

"These are the others I have mentioned to you before, Connor," Tony said.

I waited patiently for him to say more, but his mouth didn't budge as I stared at him, hoping he would explain who these people are and why was I brought here, but not a peep more came from him.

We five stood there, sharing polite-enough looks until I couldn't take any more snide glares from Cheyenne. "Okay, so what is going on?" Why was I grinning so hard?

With her arm tightly folded, Cheyenne spoke up first. "So did you tell her about us, Tony, any of it?"

"Yes, I did tell her about us, just not a lot," Tony answered, wringing his hands. He acted nervous about something, but I don't know what. "Only that she was not the only one. I thought she would take it better from a group rather than one person, Cheyenne. That way she wouldn't think I was a crazy person or something."

"Oh, this is exhausting." Cheyenne whipped her head from Tony to me and said, "You're a freak like the rest of us, okay?"

"What?" I asked. "What did she just say?" Obviously, I was not the only one surprised by what she said because Willow's mouth fell open, staring at her, and Byron walked off, shaking his head.

"Thanks, Cheyenne. That was great, just freaking awesome," Tony said, sounding not too pleased with her.

"Anytime," she said with a smirk on her face, then sat comfortably in one of the chairs.

He raised his brow to her, then said to me, "You can do things, right, besides not be seen—like run fast, able to hear a great distances, mentally move things, physically lift a house, right?"

Did he just say lift a house? It's official, I am crazy. I stood there dumbfounded and bewildered. I heard everything going on around me, but I felt stuck and unable to move.

"I told you this was a bad idea," Willow said, pacing back and forth, sounding like a mouse.

"Connor, Connor, what's wrong?" Tony said, waving his hands in front of me. "She doesn't even look like she is breathing, but her eyes are open and she is still standing. It is the strangest thing I have ever seen."

I felt cold, numb, locked inside my body. This feeling felt like it went on forever, until I finally gasped for air as if holding my breath underwater. I grabbed the closest thing next to me, which was Tony, or he grabbed me. Either way, with his help, I made it to the couch.

"What happened?" Byron asked, sitting next to me, taking my pulse. "You seemed to have gone into a catatonic state for about three minutes."

"A what?" Willow asked before I could.

Byron explained, "It is like a lack of movement or expression. It is when your body goes completely still and rigid."

"I have never done that before. I couldn't move, as if I was frozen. I felt trapped. It was weird," I said as he listened to my pulse. Willow sat on the other side of me, holding my hand.

I watched him, wondering how he knew what to do. He explained he helps with his grandfather, who is ill, and took a course in emergency care.

"Are you better now?" Byron asked, "Your vitals seem to have gone back to normal. I swear, for a minute, you didn't have a heart-beat." Once again, he answered my question before I could ask. "Your heart rate decreased significantly—well, below normal range. I say if that keeps happening, you should go get checked out."

"Okay, thanks, but I feel much better. I am sure it was just a fluke," I said. At least I hope it was.

"Now that the patient is better, Doctor, can we get back to the matter at hand?" Cheyenne said. Byron slowly glanced over at her but didn't respond. He turned back to me, smiled, then motioned for Tony to continue with a nod.

"Listen, Connor, what we are trying to say is we all have certain abilities to do the unthinkable. The other day outside, I approached you, thinking you were looking for me, remember?" Tony said, sitting across from me. "You asked how I could see you when you thought no one could. We have a glow about us that only someone like us can see."

"Show her, guys." All three of them vanished where they sat even before Tony finished asking them to. He was right. They all emitted a faint bluish color. "Maybe we do that so we can see each other," Tony said.

"Last year, Cheyenne and I found each other at a football game, and then a few months later came Byron, followed by Willow," Tony continued. "I'm figuring this didn't appear until your birthday, right?"

I had to think back. "Umm… yes, my birthday was a few months ago, and it came shortly afterward," I said.

"Well?" asked Willow. "Well, what?" I asked her.

"What can you do?" Cheyenne asked.

"I have only been able to disappear, but only twice so far. How or why is this happening, do you know?" I asked no one in particular.

"We are all still trying to figure things out. From what we gather, it occurs around your sixteenth birthday. Well, at least it did for the rest of us. I can also run really fast," Byron explained, then proceeded to run around three times, lifting up enough dust to choke a horse. He was so fast, it looked like he simply moved on from one place to another in a blink. He looked goofy when he was finished running around. He wasn't even out of breath.

Choking and waving the dust out of her face, Willow chimed in, "Um, thanks, Byron. I can electrocute, but only when electricity is available. If there was electricity in here, I would show you, but…" She trailed off, sounding upset, then spoke up again. "I'm not sure if I will be able to produce it on my own."

"Well, I can see through most objects, even flesh, and see well in the dark," Cheyenne added, clearly sounding bored. "Maybe she is broken or a half breed of some kind if invisibility is all she can do," she said, waving her arm haphazardly at me, checking out her nails.

I was about to say something not so nice to her when Tony interrupted me by cutting me off. I had just about enough of her as she sat there with a grin on her face, pleased with herself.

"Ignore Cheyenne. She will warm up to you eventually. She is always skeptical at first. Mine is strength. So nothing else then?" asked Tony.

Tony clearly didn't know me at all if he thought I cared if she warmed up to me or not. I can tell you right now being friends with her is not on my to-do list. I take back what I said earlier. It's not that she didn't have girlfriends because of the way she looks; it's because she is a witch with a capital B.

Taking my first breath after her rude statement, I decided to ignore her and turned my attention back to Tony. "No, but are we all just a bunch freaks of nature or something?" I asked.

I'm not delusional and can no longer take this lightly. I'm here in a cave, by way of an underground tunnel, under my school with people whom I don't know, and it is real. I couldn't make this up if I tried. When it was just me, I could deal with things or choose to ignore things the way I wanted, but with other people involved, I'm forced to deal with the unknown because this is much bigger than me, and I had a feeling that it was much deeper than we even knew.

Byron explained that he doesn't think this happened by chance since we all have one ability in common, but this is all still new to them. "We each have researched our families to see if we are somehow related, if our mothers were exposed to some form of radioactive experiment, or if they took the same drugs when pregnant with us, but nothing has turned up so far."

They even went as far as trying to ask their parents about strange family history, hinting to the possibility of having abilities, but each parent turned the tables and started questioning them about taking drugs so they backed off, way off.

Why do parents always pull the drug card? As if they could not possibly screw us up on their own.

"My dad even threatened to take me to a psychiatrist," Willow said.

"So bottom line, we don't know how or why this is happening to us?" I asked.

"Exactamundo," Byron said. "I am still looking into some things, but until then, we just have to lie low."

Lie low, what does that mean? Like I am going to run through the streets shouting, "I am a freak of nature!"

It just registered what Tony said earlier about it being their sixteenth birthday. "Wait, guys, I'm only fifteen. Maybe that is why my abilities are limited."

"Oh great, there goes one thing we thought we knew for sure," Willow said, slumped over in a chair like a rag doll. I didn't want to laugh at her, so I turned my head.

"Maybe hers just came early, Willow, and when her sixteenth birthday comes along, so will all her abilities," Byron said to her. The way he spoke to her gave me the impression they were more than friends.

"So I say we keep looking into our family's pasts and see if anything turns up. You never know, maybe something will pop up. Sorry, Connor, wish we had more answers for you, but now you, being another body, can look into your family's history as well. More heads are better than one," Byron said.

"True. I want to find out what is going on. Do you think there are others like us?" I asked him.

"If there are, hopefully they will show themselves to us or do something foolish like rat us out somehow, even if it is not done on purpose either way. Be careful," Byron said.

We all agreed and decided to end for the night. Cheyenne had to talk to Tony about something for a minute before we parted ways.

I had a feeling about them too. Maybe that is why she was giving me the stare down. If they have a thing going on, it is up to Tony to tell me.

We all left at the same time. Tony and I were the only ones that went in the same direction on foot. The other three left together in a nice SUV, a black Range Rover. Byron got behind the wheel, so I assumed it was his car. How nice for him. I cannot wait to turn sixteen so I can get my license, then I could at least drive my parents' car.

We took our time walking and talking not wanting to rush home; at least I didn't, and he seemed okay with that.

"What do you think? Did we scare you off?" he asked. "Surprisingly, I'm okay. For a minute, it was touch and go. I am more curious at this point. Sorry I went all

rigid on you in there," I said.

"It's cool. I didn't know what to expect. I'm just glad you didn't run off screaming," he said.

I almost did, little did he know the only thing that stopped me was my catatonic state of mind.

I'm still at a loss about that one. I have never done that before. Maybe I had a mini stroke, who knows.

"Hey, how come I've never seen the others before?" I asked.

"They go to a school out of town about thirty minutes away. We are the only two that go to Randell High."

"How often do you guys meet up?" I asked, curious about their meeting arrangements. "Is this a monthly thing?"

"We meet up only when we need to. By the way, here's my cell number. You know, just in case something comes up," Tony said, handing me my cell phone back that I didn't notice he took in the first place. He practically shoved it in my hand, then walked up.

I stopped walking, looked at my cell, then back at him. Suppressing a bewildered smile, I caught up to him when he slowed down enough for me to catch up.

"Sure, thanks, but I'm not going to ask how you got it," I said, stone faced. I attempted to give him my number too, but he explained he had it already. I asked how he got my number, and he said, "If I told you, then I would have to kill you."

Somebody watches way too many spy movies. "So I guess we will keep prying into things, huh?" I asked.

"Yes, we will. Hopefully, I didn't make things worse by bringing you here first before telling you about us," Tony said.

I couldn't see his face, but I heard the sincerity in his voice and told him that it was fine. I wanted him to feel better, so I said, "I probably would have thought you were crazy." In the big scheme of things, now that reality has slapped me in the face, I am glad there are others, and that in itself was comforting.

We walked and talked about other things the rest of the way home. I asked him why I never saw in him in school before this year. He explained I have and that we have had classes together, but I never paid him any attention. He was trying to explain who he was, but I couldn't remember him until he said he was the skinny boy with braces who sat behind Cricket in math class last year.

I laughed so hard tears streamed down my face when I remembered who he was. We used to call him Peewee in elementary school—he was so skinny. He didn't find it particularly funny, but I did. I asked him what he did to get so buff and tall.

"I was this tall last year, thank you, but you never noticed. I got my braces off, finally, and went through a major outward growth spurt soon after I turned sixteen. I work out, but honestly, I didn't do much. I worked on my skateboarding skills, and the abilities came with some added benefits. This year, I came back as a new man," he said, asking me to feel his muscles as he flexed.

I laughed and apologized, then laughed some more and apologized again every time I thought of how awkward he was. He made fun of himself too. I told him of some not-so-flattering stories of myself too. Before I knew it, I was home.

I thought it was nice that he walked me all the way home. Wow, he is cute and courteous, nice. I still wondered what was up with him and Cheyenne. Maybe I'll ask him the next time I see him, who knows.

Chapter 7

For the next few days, I lived and breathed in detective mode. I searched all over the house for any questionable family history. I dug through old letters, some paperwork, even an old rusty locked box that had old baseball cars in them but found nothing.

Weeks went by and Tony and I passed each other in the halls with no more than a slight glance. We decided to play it cool for now, not do anything out of the ordinary to make our friends ask any questions, especially Angela.

That was partly true; the other reason is I didn't want to stay hung up on a guy who may have a girlfriend. I didn't feel it was my place to ask, so I kept my distance even though I really wanted to hang out with him during school.

Like usual, he hung with the individuals who did the sports thing, not your typical football or basketball. The only sport he would do in school was swim like me. He liked cycling and surfing. He was good at it and won most local competitions. Geez, I wonder why. He was major-league built, not huge or anything yucky, but lean and muscular.

After school was a different story. Every day during swim practice, the male and female teams competed with each other. My coach wanted to push us harder, so she was adamant about pairing us, and as luck would have it, I paired with Tony. It was not so much as luck, as we were both captain of our swim teams. Each year, the spot of captain went to the fastest swimmer and who won the most competitions the year before.

He seemed to like that we paired together as much as I did, so why didn't he say anything about Cheyenne? It was frustrating trying to figure him out. I couldn't tell my friends about him, so I couldn't talk to anyone about him. This sucked.

Every day after practice and before my parents got home, I would search their room and my dad's office.

On this particular evening after school, while babysitting Reptile Boy, I almost went blind when I stumbled upon my dad's dirty magazines. Gross, Dad, you are way too old for this stuff.

Then I stumbled across my mom's naughty wear. Okay, now I am officially blind. I most definitely needed therapy.

What were they thinking?

I decided to call the bedroom quits and try my parents' office upstairs instead for the millionth time. I searched for loose floorboards, under drawers, behind the desk. I mean I dug everywhere. I grabbed a file off the desk right when I heard someone come up behind me.

"What are you doing? You know you are not supposed to be in here. I'm going to tell." It was Reptile Boy peeping in from the doorway, too scared to come in. This room was off-limits.

"Oh, shut up. Go away, you…"

Slam!

The door shut in his face as if I wished it would in my head. I stood frozen in the middle of the room in awe, listening to him yell at me from the hallway.

"You shut the door in my face with your long monkey arms," he whined from the other side. He tried to get back in, but it wouldn't budge. The knob twisted and turned as he tugged on it but refused to open.

Standing there still frozen, unlike the way frozen in the tunnel, not wanting to move but pondering what just happened. From here, I could see the door was clearly not locked, yet it would not open.

Could I be doing that?

I took a slow deep breath, allowing myself to relax my thoughts when Kane practically flew through the door. He must have put all his weight into it, not expecting it to open, then tripped over his left foot, hitting the floor hard.

He scurried off the floor, rubbed his nose, and said, "You alien with long monkey arms! I'm telling Mom you're in this office and that you hit me with the door."

He rambled on about something, but I inadvertently tuned him out. Under normal circumstances, I would have laughed myself into hysteria when he fell, but there was nothing normal about these circumstances. All I could think of was the possibility of me shutting the door in my brother's face from the middle of my parents' office.

Next thing I heard was the front door closing, which brought me back to reality, and Kane whining all the way downstairs. "Mom, Connor..."

Seriously, that kid doesn't skip a beat. Attempting to put things back where they were, I overheard him whining about where I was and what cruelty I forced upon him by hitting his nose with the door. What a menace, always getting me into trouble.

"Connor," my mom said from the front room below.

"Yes," I said, slipping into the hall quietly, trying to shut the door.

"Come down please," she said.

Somewhat in a daze, I somehow managed to make my way down to the kitchen. She was fumbling through the fridge, looking for what she was going to make for dinner.

I don't know why my mom wears heels and a dress suit every day to work when she has to wear a lab coat. If I were her, it would be comfortable jeans day every day.

"Did you slam the door in your brother's face, and were you in the office?" she asked, pulling out some meat and stared at me.

What was I going to say—no, it was a figment of his imagination, or the wind did it? So I owned up to it.

"Don't slam the door in your brother's face, and stay out of that office please. You know we have important papers in there," she said, pissed.

Rolling my eyes, I said, "Not to me. I mean, sure." I tried to suppress a grin, failing miserably. She gave me that look parents give that says, "You're pushing it," while trying to console the little reptilian who was holding on to her leg for dear life.

Little brothers are so annoying and dramatic. Thank goodness for kids' rationalization of things. If he were more aware, he would have realized I was about ten feet from the door so I could not have reached it. Also, my hands were holding some files.

After ten seconds of the stare down, I turned to leave. I wanted to call Tony and tell him the good news when she stopped me first pivot.

"Where are you going, young lady? Turn right back around and get dinner started, and next time, do it as soon as you get in. You know the rule: whoever is home first starts dinner. Is your homework done?" she snapped at me. She hates it when I roll my eyes, but sometimes they just do it on their own. I cannot control all my bodily movements.

"Why do I have to start dinner all the time? Queen Precious is never here to do any work, and yes, I finished my homework in free period. It's in the den on the table like always," I said, frustrated that my parents constantly stay on me about my schoolwork. It's seriously annoying. Well, it is my fault, but still they could ease up.

"If you were in a sport that ran late a lot, then you would not be here either, but you are, so get started. I will look your homework over in a bit," she said, pointing to the stove.

"I didn't know making out was a sport," I said, stomping hard toward the kitchen counter and slapping the package of meat over to open it, portraying the role of the abused brat.

"Do that over the sink and watch your mouth, Connor. We say nothing when your swim meets run late either. Your sister is cheer captain, and the big game is this weekend. You should try out for cheerleading next year. I'm sure you would be great. You have such a tiny frame for the pyramid, and you don't seem to fear anything, especially with that mouth of yours."

I would rather die first. "I don't do cults, and I'm not drinking the Kool-Aid," I yelled to her as she headed up the stairs to shower and change.

"Connor, you are way too young to be so cynical!" she yelled back, trying to still sound pissed, but I heard humor in her tone. She knows I'm right. They take cheer to a whole other level. Constantly practicing, having to wear the school colors of red and white daily and at private meetings. Please, they are probably out terrorizing little children as we speak.

Reptile Boy stood there the whole time, grinning at me. I stuck my tongue out at him, and he ran off. What a brat.

Chapter 8

Dinner was exceptionally brutal, sitting with my parents, trying to make small talk. All I wanted to do was break into song and dance from the excitement of a possible ability. Right after dinner finished, I rushed to my room and called Tony to tell him the good news.

"I knew you couldn't hold out much longer. You miss me, don't you?" he said. "Okay, okay, tell me what happened." "Yes, you're right. You're all I think about night and day," I said. "No, seriously, my abilities may be developing." I told him what happened about three times. I couldn't

stop myself, my mouth was going a mile a minute. "Cool, that's awesome. Hey, how about I come by in about an hour so you can show me?" he asked.

"What, um, sure," I said, jumping off the bed to try to find something nice to wear. That was a challenge for me. Everything I owned just about had some sci-fi connotation or simply jeans and T-shirts.

"I feel an hour is plenty enough time for you to put on your cute jammies," Tony said and hung up before I could say a word. He thought he was so funny.

I was scrambling to find something decent to put on, but wearing my brother's pajamas would show him I didn't care. Yes, it is sad that I can still fit some of his clothes.

Who was I kidding? Tony was adorably cute. Okay, seriously, he was a doll with those long eyelashes above those light brown eyes and the way he smirks when he looks back at me...

"Connor!" my mom yelled from downstairs, yanking me right out of my lovely daydream. Snap out of it, Connor. The first boy that shows you attention, you get all giddy.

"Yes, Mom," I said, so not wanting to answer back. "Come clean up the kitchen. Your sister is not back

yet. Practice ran later than expected," she said.

"No, it didn't. She knows exactly what time to come back so she won't have to clean," I barked back, knowing full well Ebony is full of crap. She pulls this all the time, and they let her get away with it.

"I will talk to her later about it. Just come down here and finish up. We already did most of it. I have to get your brother ready for bed," she said.

She has the worst timing. I ran down the stairs, rushing to the kitchen, causing my dad to yell something about not running down the stairs. I grabbed the broom and got busy. My mom thanked me with a kiss on the forehead then rushed off. They didn't leave me that much to do, so I quickly cleaned up what was left and had thirty minutes to spare.

Tap, tap, tap.

No way. Please don't let that be Tony knocking at my back door already. Sure enough, there he was, standing on my deck with a nauseating grin. The shade on the back door was open, so he got full view of my ensemble.

My hair was a mess because strands of it hung down across my face, and of course, I had on old comfortable clothes. The kind you seriously don't want anyone to see you in except your family.

With my head hung low, I walked over to the door and opened it, "You said in an hour? I have thirty minutes to spare, man," I said, giving him the cold stare. He leaned against the doorsill, enjoying this way too much for my liking. I know he showed up early on purpose.

"I thought to myself, why wait and pass up the opportunity to see your latest fashion of home wear? I was simply hoping for something cute or maybe a superhero costume, but what you have on now has a certain homeless flair that goes beyond mine or anybody else's wildest imagination."

I sighed, rolled my eyes, and said, "Let it go, man. Let it go." After telling him to stay put, I ran upstairs to change.

A pair of dark jeans, a sparkly black tank top, and ten minutes later, I shut my bedroom door behind me. On the way down, I peeked in on Kane and found him sleeping at the foot of his bed, so I turned him around and tucked him in. He is so cute and innocent when he slept; awake was a different story. After checking on my parents to make sure they were in for the night, I headed out back down.

As I have said before, Ebony will sneak in later. "Tony, Tony, where are you?" I whispered, searching

the yard for him, but he was nowhere. I figured he would be on the deck like last time.

There were several hideouts in my backyard, and he must have found one. Going down the deck steps to search for him, I couldn't help but wonder, do boys ever grow up?

"Toneeee!" I squealed, when he sprang out and grabbed me from behind. "Grow up already!" Glad I wasn't gassy, or it could have gotten ugly.

He was hiding behind the gazebo in between the flowerbed and bushes, just like my little brother does to terrorize Ebony when her boyfriend, Robert, comes over. With her, it's funny; now not so much.

"You are crazy, you know that? Your mother should have you tested," I said, pulling myself together. He scared the crap out of me.

I couldn't stay mad at him for too long. He looked nice in his baggy, but not too baggy, dark jeans, gray T-shirt with some emblem in it, and a silver bracelet that stood out against his caramel complexion. He stood about a foot taller than me. Who doesn't though?

He just stood there as if he was waiting for something, then said, "So let's see it."

"What a way to put a girl on the spot. I don't think I can just turn it off and on like talking about it," I said.

"You have to practice at it. That is how we learned on command. Try to see what you can do. Let's see," he said, stepping back, searching for something. "Focus on that branch over there." He pointed to a small branch about ten feet away from us.

I was hesitant but attempted it anyway. I turned toward the branch and focused on it hard, but it didn't move at all.

"I think you are trying too hard. Your body tends to show what you're feeling, so relax your face and hands," Tony said. I did as he suggested. "Now try again."

I stared hard, telling it to float in my head. About a minute later, still nothing.

"That's okay, breathe. What were you doing when the door suddenly closed?" Tony asked.

"I was in my parents' office when my brother showed up. I was thinking I wish the door would shut in his face so he could leave," I said.

"So how were you feeling?" he asked. "Annoyed, agitated," I said, shrugging not sure.

"Emotional then, maybe that is your thing. Cheyenne, Willow, and I were that way too. Emotions controlled our abilities in the beginning. Byron, well, he is always calm. Mine was associated with anger until I learned to control it through a lot of practice. We all had to practice. At times Willow's emotions still get to her," Tony explained.

"Try this: close your eyes and block out everything around you. Recreate those same emotions and contain them. See the branch in your head first, then imagine it moving. Next, open your eyes to focus on that branch only," he said.

I turned away from him as he spoke, then closed my eyes to block out everything else. I thought about how I felt at that moment upstairs, opened my eyes, focused on the branch, but still nothing.

"It's not working. Maybe I didn't really close the door. Maybe the wind blew it shut. Maybe I made it all up," I said, feeling deflated.

"Don't give up so quickly. Try not to only feel the emotions, but let them build up in you and take over your doubts and those fears of negativity you're holding on to, blocking your flow of energy." He walked around me as he spoke. "Allow the positive energy to flow around you, through you." His voice was soothing, helping me relax, letting me travel to an inner sense of balance I never knew I had. My breathing slowed considerably. My muscles loosened, detaching from me, allowing my mind to levitate. My senses were alive, but I felt and heard nothing around me, only the wind.

I felt happiness earlier in the room, not annoyance or frustration, so I let those emotions swallow me. In my mind, I pictured the branch move off the ground. Staying in that moment, still controlling my breathing, I slowly opened my eyes and saw nothing but the branch. At first, it started to shake, then it elevated until it was eye level with me.

It just stayed there, not moving; and neither did I, afraid it may drop or, worse, fly off.

I could hear Tony telling me to hold it steady now, see if I could make it come to me. He sounded far away, a million miles away.

"Who's there?"

Shoot, it was my sister Ebony. The branch dropped at the same time we hit the ground. We took cover behind the same bush he hid from me and stayed quiet as a mouse. Neither one of us heard Robert's car pull up.

Please don't let her catch me or I will be grounded for life. I was just thankful we kept the gazebo lights off.

"Who's there? I swear I heard something, Robert," Ebony said.

"No one is out here, babe. What you heard was my heart aching for your love. Let's finish what we started earlier," Robert said in an unusually deep voice.

I vomited a little in my mouth. How cheesy was that line? I turned to mouth something sarcastic to Tony, but he was too busy trying not to crack up. I had to cover his mouth and pin him down to stop him from rolling around on the grass, dying of laughter.

"Back off, Robert, I told you I am not doing that. A guy has to put a ring on this finger before anything else," Ebony said.

"Oh, come on. Do you know how many girls would love to be in your shoes? A guy has needs, you know," Robert said.

Could it be that my sister is still a good girl? Have I been wrong all these years? I lifted my head a little in order to peep through the bushes past the gazebo so I could see what was going on. My head was so awkwardly cocked that I'm sure resembled a chicken, but this was good stuff. Robert had Ebony pinned against the house.

"I am sure Patricia would love to be in my shoes. If you are so inclined, go call her. She is always chasing after you anyway," Ebony said, easing inside the house, slamming the door in his face.

"But, baby…" were the last few words Robert got out before she slammed the door in his face. He pressed his head against the door, lightly tapping it with a fist a few seconds longer, then walked off toward the front of the house with his head hung low.

I waited until I heard his car drive off before moving another muscle.

"So jock Robert has no game, huh?" Tony said, still cracking up.

What Tony found hilarious, I found shocking. I thought for sure Ebony and Robert went way past kissing. I was somewhat proud of her, but it lasted only a minute and quickly got over it.

We chilled, sitting still a while longer until we figured the coast was clear. Tony whispered. "You did it. This is amazing. What do they call it again, telekinesis? I'd pick it if I had a choice." He gave a high five, congratulating me.

I was overjoyed, even speechless, and that was major for me not to have anything to say. All I could do was gloat. I did it, and it felt wonderful.

Chapter 9

We practiced and practiced, time flying by, and before we knew it, it was 3:00 a.m. on a school morning. I was only going to get about four hours of sleep, but it was worth it. We decided to call it a night.

"We should meet up like this more often to practice," I suggested. "I need some catching up to do."

"Yeah, the rest of us used to meet, but then we concentrated more on finding out about how we happened. Eventually, our practice lessons slowed down until they completely stopped, you know," he said, leaning against the gazebo, twirling some grass in his hands.

"Hey, did this ever scare you? I mean, did it feel wrong, or were you just okay with it?" I asked, not able to keep my arms still, still gloating, so I crossed them as I stood across from Tony.

"I was always okay with it, calm when it came. It felt right to me, as if I finally found what had always been missing, the true me. As a kid,

I always felt different, you know. That's why I got into trouble a lot. My dad did say I was always looking for trouble." He smiled. "Not trouble, Pops, just me." I had a feeling that last statement was not for me but what he would like to say to his dad. I stood there waiting as he stared off, deep in thought. "It was the other three that seem to have an issue. You?" he asked.

"I was actually fine with it and wanted more of it. That is, until the night I met the others. Meeting them made it real to me, forcing me to face that this is bigger than just I am. In the beginning, I didn't think through the seriousness of it," I said.

"I feel you," he said. "For a while, I was getting bummed out about this business. The others never seemed to get into it as much, so I played it cool. Now that you came along, it feels new again, you know, so meeting up sounds good to me."

"I do, trust me."

"Cool, but remember, be careful. We don't know who else may be involved. See you in school tomorrow. I might even say hello to you. You never know," Tony said.

"Oh please, you have been dying to talk to me."
I stood there arms still folded, trying hard to act
cool when he stepped to me and leaned in close
to my face. Oh, is he going to kiss me? This is it. I
swallowed hard, held my breath, and closed my
eyes preparing for it.

Feeling his warm breath on my face, he kissed
my forehead. "I have seen you checking me out.
You can't keep your eyes off this." He gestured
toward his body, rubbing his chest with an obnoxious leer that made me want to smack him.
As if that was not bad enough, he had the nerve
to wink at me.

That was it. It is official. I hate little boys
and their silly little jokes. He obviously amuses
himself, so why do I need to stick around and
be a spectator? On that note, I abruptly turned
around and walked off, somewhat embarrassed
for being too eager and offended by the game. He
was not going to ruin my overall blissful night.

"Come on, Connor, I was playing with…" I
didn't even hear the rest. The door shut before he
finished his sentence, and by the time I reached
the top step, my grin was back.

"Why are you grinning like that? Where were you? You were out back with some boy, weren't you?" Ebony attacked me at the top of the stairs; she was practically in my face so I had to step back. Where did she leap from, the ceiling? Ugh, what a way to ruin a night.

"What's with the interrogation? I don't have to…," I said, attempting to get a word in.

"I bet you were. Listen, Connor." She sighed, "I know you don't know much about boys, but you cannot let them have their way. They should treat you like a lady." She reached for my hands. Was she seriously trying to be a civilized human being to me, an actual big sister? Yet somehow, when she does, it comes out Stepford-like, robotic, and simply unnatural. I was slightly scared for my life, not really, but it was impossible for me to take her seriously.

"I was not out with some boy. I was in the basement studying." Good one. I do that from time to time. She never goes down there. One scary movie about basements, and she has been done with them ever since she was a kid.

"Good, because I don't want to go to a school where my sister has a bad reputation. I would hate for you to have to switch schools," she said, trying to sound sincere.

Well, there went that tender moment. First off, I would not switch schools even if I had a reputation, simply for her sake. I would stay there and make her life miserable. I stepped back from her again and folded my arms for the second time tonight, but this time it was out of sheer annoyance.

"I'm only looking out for you," she said in a high-pitched tone, sounding offended that I snubbed her affections and advice.

She is so self-centered. No matter what is going on in your life, somehow she turns it around to make it about her. The sad part is she doesn't even realize it.

"Yes, Ebony, I am feeling all tingly inside from this oh-so-touching, moving moment," I said as I clutched my heart with my right hand, gracefully placed my left hand against my forehead, and fell against the wall, mocking her.

"Oh, you are so dramatic. You really need to grow up," she said, walking off.

After that, I got ready for bed but barely slept that night. All I could think about was finally for the first time in my life, I, Connor Esquibel, am not just the middle kid but somebody extraordinary.

I thought about telling Angela and Hope, but would they understand and how much would I tell them? What answers could I give them?

What if they thought I was weird or somehow found out about the others? No, I will wait until I knew more. I felt so guilty not telling them. In due time, I told myself, and I drifted off to sleep.

Chapter 10

The next day at school was the same as every other day. Madness. I watched people dash to and from classes, the lunchroom, hearing lockers slam as students hurry off to their next destination or, for some, begrudgingly, to the principal's office for their daily scolding with such intensity, but not me. Still in good spirits from last night, I was strolling along on cloud nine.

Like usual we, meaning Angela, Hope, and her boyfriend, Stoney, and I were hanging out by the lockers between our next classes, getting out books when Angela asked why I was so chipper. Usually, Angela's boyfriend Bobby would be with us, but he was working on a science project today.

"I told you, guys, she has a man. You little sneak. Who is he? Does he go to our school? Why are you holding out?" Angela was about to lose her mind not being in the know, gripping her books so tightly, I swear I heard "Help me." I protested and swore it's not true, right when someone walked over midsentence interrupting me. "Hey, Connor, what's up?" Flinching, I turned around, and it was none other than Tony. His right shoulder parked it against the locker next to mine. He smelled nice as usual, not that I cared, after last night's joke on my behalf.

Could he not have picked a better time? Great. Now they are going to ask me crazy amount of questions.

"Hey, what's up, funny man?" I said, refusing to look at him but in my locker as if it captivated me with the mind-blowing wonders it held of photos, books, and notes. Knowing full well, he waited until all my friends were around to come over.

"You left your book behind after class today." He handed me an unrecognizable book, but there was a note sticking out the top. I grabbed the book and pushed the note down quickly so nosy 1, 2, and 3 wouldn't see it.

"Hey, thanks. I didn't realize I left it," I said with a raised eyebrow, giving him the stink eye. I guess texting was out of the question, I thought, hoping he could read my mind.

Angie stepped so close to him, she broke all personal space rules, practically pinning him against the locker, eyes about to pop out of her head, turning on the charm. "Hello, I'm Angela. This is Hope, and in the rear is Stoney. We call him Step because he is the best on the step team." If she smiled any harder, we could see all her teeth, even the ones in the back. I think she was actually salivating from this unexpected turn of events, proving she had been right all along that I had been hiding a boyfriend from them.

Hellos were said, and the guys did their hand dap thing. Tony seemed to be taking it in stride where I would have made my exit a while ago. Why are my friends so embarrassing?

"I didn't know you and Connor were in any classes together. Which class is it, exactly?" Angela grilled on.

"Back off, Angie, like you know everyone in my classes," I said, trying to push her back, but her feet were rooted firmly onto the ground, not moving.

"Being that I'm in most of them, I should know," she said, not skipping a beat when she answered me but continued to stare at Tony. "So which class were you saying?" Oh, help me, she is in journalist mode. The other two in the back were useless, just letting her run with it.

I nudged her back harder now, threw the book in the locker, thanked Tony, and turned to walk off. Angie yanked me back by my waist and held on to me. I looked down at the floor, hoping it would somehow open up and swallow me.

"We're not in any classes together. She takes a class before me. Our moms know each other," Tony graciously said. I turned to face at him, like the rest of the vultures behind me, and mouthed, "Good one."

"See you around, Sci-fi," he winked back with that oh-so-devilish grin of his, strolling off.

"Seriously," I said, before I knew it, not playing that one off at all.

"He is cute, Sci-fi. Didn't know you liked the athletic type," Hope said. "Maybe we can do a triple date?" Hope and Angela ran with that idea about where, when, even outfits were discussed. I had to put a stop to it and quick.

"Wait a minute, guys, Tony and I are just friends. Besides, he has never asked me out, so cool it." It's true we are just friends, and he may have a girl. I didn't tell them that, or that would have been another big deal.

"Oh please, it is obvious he's into you. The way he strolled over to you, grinning like that. Trust me, I know what I am talking about. Why don't I go talk to him and set this straight?" Angela said as if she came up with the most brilliant idea ever.

"You're too pushy, Angie, and you're no better, Hope. Stoney, help," I begged.

Stoney took his leave. "Sorry, ladies, I am out of here. This girl drama is not my thing."

Yeah, that's questionable. I slammed my locker shut and said, "Absolutely not both of you. Just leave Tony alone." I realized they were not listening to me but instead staring past me with astonished expressions on their faces.

I turned around to see what was so mesmerizing. They were staring at my locker pushed inward from my own doing. I broke my locker without even trying. Oh crap, what do I even say? I planted my face against it and sulked.

Someone touched my back. I slowly turned back around to see it was Hope. I stood there, not knowing what to say as they stared at me like

I was some sick puppy. Cautiously, Hope spoke up first. "It's okay, Connor, we will leave Tony alone. We didn't mean to upset you. Is your hand okay?"

Angela reached for my hand, but I pulled away and pretended to wince. What else was I supposed to do? Now they're going to think I'm some crazy person. They kept gawking at me. What do I do? What do I say as we just stood there? I was at a loss for words.

The bell finally rang, thank goodness; the period between classes was over. I told them I'm going to the nurse and would see them later. Feeling eyes on the back of my head as I, for the first time today, hurried up. Like Tony said last night, we need to be careful.

I practically had to beg the nurse to wrap my hand, even though she didn't see anything wrong with it. I told her it would help me psychologically, but I'm sure what she would rather do is get me psychologically tested. She wrapped, I pretended to wince, and off to classes I went.

Chapter 11

Once I left the nurse's office, I went straight to the principal's office and explained to Mrs. Potts, the office administrator, that my locker had a huge dent in the middle of it skipping the "I did it" part to the "I don't have a clue" ending.

The expression she gave me told me she didn't believe me at all, but since no further explanation came, she eventually got up and told the vice principal, who said he would look into it but for now to call environmental services.

When she opened the principal's door, I saw he had company as usual. I glanced at her desk and saw she had some files of, I'm sure, the repeat offenders. When she returned, I thanked her then took my leave.

Instead of heading straight to my next class, I headed back to my locker, feeling compelled to go back for the book Tony gave me. At the scene of the crime where my locker was murdered by my own doing, I carefully opened it, retrieving the book and pulled out the note. What was so important that Tony could not wait to give me or call me later about it?

We are meeting again this Friday, two days away. What is with Fridays? I'm screwed. Stoney's step team has a big competition that night, and we had plans to go out after. Once again, I will have to make an excuse and bail out afterward.

"Back to class, Connor," I heard someone say to the left of me. It was Ronald, the hall monitor. You have to love them; if it were not for hall monitors and their authority, schools would be in such chaos. I laughed aloud, not meaning to, and was met with an ugly expression of disapproval.

I gently closed the locker, waved good-bye to Ronald, who was walking off while jotting in his notepad, something about my locker no doubt, then took off running toward my next class.

My run was cut short when I bumped into the same grungy kid who had been watching us last week on our way to the lunchroom. The one Hope not so discreetly pointed out.

"Sorry, I didn't see you there," I apologized, backing up. He had the same scowl on his face like last week. He didn't say anything as I bent down to pick up my note.

Something strange about him caught my eye. He was standing in front of me, glowing. His, a faint grayish glow unlike our blue, was glowing brighter and brighter.

Why is he even glowing? Then it hit me that the hall monitor didn't say anything to him because he couldn't see him; only I could as the others showed me the first night we met in the cave. A chill ran up my spine. I stood up quickly. I had a bad feeling about him.

We lingered there, staring at each other, not moving. It started to feel hot and uncomfortable in the hallway. I could smell him and could see the beads of sweat dripping off him. He breathed so loudly, it frustrated me.

His eyes glowed light brown to almost transparent; that's when something inside me took over. I slammed him up against the locker with one arm and told him to stay away from me or he would regret it.

I don't know what came over me, but I couldn't help it. I didn't want to help it. I liked it. A burst of energy exploded inside of me, causing havoc to my organs. Everything rapidly churned faster and faster. I thought my body would explode right until I couldn't take it anymore, then finally a rush ran through me. For a minute, I felt high, light-headed, allowing him to get the best of me.

He flipped me so quickly, my back was against the locker. He punched me in the gut, but then I kicked him in the groin. He let go of me, doubling over, so I uppercut him in the chin. He flew off his feet, hit the floor hard, and slid to the other side of the hallway, slamming his head into a locker. I ran over to him, but he managed to kick my legs up from under me. I fell back, knocking my head against the tile floor.

He picked me up by my collar and slammed me against the locker again and said, "Not before I kill you first. You and your boyfriend Tony," then he threw me down the hall, but before I could get up, he was gone.

I was trying to slow my breathing down and control my rage. My hands fisted and ready to pounce anything that came my way. I took my frustration it out on the nearest locker, denting another one.

Realizing what I did, I checked my surroundings, and luckily, no one was around. How did no one hear that?

I grabbed my phone to message Tony, telling him I needed to see him ASAP. We agreed to meet in the haunted bathroom after school.

I went to the nearest restroom to check myself, but I was fine, not a scratch or a bruise anywhere on my body. I managed to pull it together long enough to finish my last two classes of the day. By the time the second class ended, I felt more like myself.

I messaged Angela and told her I had a project to do after school and would call her later. She tried calling me, but I refused to answer and subject myself to unanswerable questions. She sent me a message she wanted to meet, but I told her again I would call her later.

Tony met me in the bathroom as promised, but we decided it was better to go the cave so we didn't have to worry about anyone overhearing us. We decided it was best to go undetected as we headed to the cave. We made sure no one was around when we opened the door to sneak in the boiler room. Mr. Johnston was not here, thank goodness.

Making it to the cave, Tony sat me down and asked me to explain from the beginning; he sounded more worried than I did. "What exactly happened? I even want the tiniest details."

I started from the beginning and told him all I remembered, even confessed my locker crime.

"Where was he coming from, and why didn't you tell me some guy was watching you?" he asked.

"I'm not sure which direction he came from, only he was there. I do not know for sure he has been watching me, only that one time he was watching me, if that makes any sense," I said.

He was pacing back and forth. "We knew there would be others out there, but I never sensed him," Tony said.

"He can't be like us, right, because his glow was different, right? Maybe we can only sense each other and not others unlike us." This was the craziest conversation I have ever had, "others like us" or "unlike us."

"Connor, can you sense me?" he asked. "What?" I asked, half paying attention.

"Can you sense me? Do you know when I am around?" he asked.

"No, maybe because I'm new to my abilities and they're not fully developed yet," I said.

"Okay, think back. The day we met at school, why did you come outside?" he asked with such seriousness.

"Because I wanted to leave." It made sense to me. "Anything else?" he asked.

"I just had a strong urge to, I guess." "What did that urge feel like?" he asked.

"It felt like a pull or strong desire, why? What does it feel like to you?"

"I guess the same way, but since it has happened to me a few times already, I know it is coming from one of us," he explained.

"Maybe he is like us but different, if that makes any sense. Oh, wait a minute," I said, standing up walking closer to Tony. "I did have a strong urge to return to my locker, but maybe the urge was this kid. He was by my locker, and funny I ran in that direction afterward. I could have easily gone the other way. Actually, I should have, it would have taken less time to get to class. It was the same feeling when I met you."

"Then that is it. It doesn't make anything definite about him, but, Connor, you have to be more careful especially after the locker incident. What was that about?" Tony asked.

"Girl stuff." I was not giving him the full scoop. "I don't know. It just happened. I have slammed that locker a million times, and that has never happened before. I guess we have to be more conscientious now." Then it clicked. "Tony, how does he know about you? I mean, I saw him when Ronald couldn't, so he knew I was different, but you?"

"I have a feeling he knew about us long before you saw him today, Connor, or at least suspected. Otherwise, he would not have been watching you last week or been by your locker today."

"We have to be more careful and more concerned as to who else is out there," Tony said, then started mumbling aloud to himself, deep in thought again.

He turned his attention back to me. "I want to meet him, this kid. You need to point him out to me. He may be able to give us some answers, or at the least, more heads are better than one. You get the concept. Well, ask him questions after I pound his face in first. Why didn't he come to me?"

Tony was adamant and beyond pissed, but after talking some sense into him, he finally compromised after calming down. We decided to talk to the others about it on Friday.

Later that night from home, I called Angela and Hope on three-way to explain everything was fine. After a million questions, they relaxed and decided they would not sell me to the circus and make money off me as the strongest woman alive. We laughed about it and said it was probably a fluke, and that was that.

This may be tougher than I thought. I hated lying to my friends, but if they freaked over a locker incident, just think how they would react if they knew everything. I felt it best not to let them in on my secret, at least for now. Plus, after what went down today in school, it would only put them in danger.

Chapter 12

Friday night came, and the step competition was in full force. It was the big division battle, and we were up against last year's rival. They swore we only beat them only by one point or we cheated somehow. This past year, our team worked extra hard and came up with some new moves.

Stoney had a solo, and he owned it. The crowd was rowdy as he put on a show. He was overly animated, which clued some of us in about his questionable sexuality, but Hope as usual didn't get the hint. She screamed "That's my man," while Angela, Bobby, and some others exchanged glances, then cheered right on.

Once again, like last year, we blew them out the water. We won for the fourth season in a row. Our archnemesis came in second. They are actually good, but we won't tell them that.

After the competition was over, we met up with Stoney, tonight's Mr. MVP, and a few others to decide where we were going to grub. If I was hungry, I know they were starving, but then again, when am I not hungry? I was about to suggest a place when I remembered tonight's meeting in the cave with Tony and the others at eleven.

It was already ten thirty, and I hadn't even thought up an excuse to give. I rode with Angela here, but I couldn't tell her to drop me off at the school. No excuse in the world could explain that one, so walking there was the only option. The school was only a few blocks away, but I needed to get going to make it there on time.

"What's wrong, Connor? You look confused," Angela asked. I really need to control my facial expressions.

I was about to blurt something unbelievable out when Tony came over. He probably didn't even know it, but he saved me from an interrogation of the worst kind.

"Hey, Connor. What's up, guys?" Tony said, acknowledging the boys on the team. They obviously knew each other according to what the conversation entailed. After the boys finished grunting and making odd noises, which seems so caveman like, Tony turned his attention back to me. "Sorry, I'm late, but it was virtually impossible to muscle through this crowd. Don't be mad." Then he leaned in and gave me a kiss on the cheek.

I must have had the stupidest look on my face to make Hope nudge some sense into me. "Oh that's... huh...

what... that's okay, I totally understand. I wasn't sure if you were really going to show up or not," I said, stumbling over my words, as if English was not my primary language. From the corner of my eye, I could see the girls laughing at me.

"I got to represent. I think everyone from school is here. Besides, I had to see how the commoners compete, being an extremist myself, of course," he said, giving the guys a hard time. They went back and forth, giving each other crap for a minute until someone remembered food.

I was about to say we can't, but Tony cut me off. "That's cool, Connor, do you want to ride with me?"

I refused to look at either Hope or Angela and said yes. He was throwing me off; obviously, he had to tell me something. Maybe the meeting was canceled, which was fine with me. Fridays are for going out.

We decided to meet up at our favorite burger joint, Juicy Burger, then went our separate ways to our modes of transportation. I was about to ask him something when he shook his head no.

Walking to his car in silence, I wondered, did something happen to one of the others? He steered me toward a midnight-blue racer-striped 2011 Ford Mustang Shelby GT500. This is one of my top favorite cars ever. I fell, no, I melted against it. "Is this mine?" That accidentally slipped out, but that didn't stop me from hugging the car.

He blinked a few times, then said, "No, it's mine, and if it goes missing, I'm coming for you. Please get off the hood and get in the car so we can go." I said just kidding, trying to play if off, but first chance, this car is mine.

"So I guess you like her, huh?" he asked, spinning out the lot, showing off how fast she can go.

"She is only one of the hottest cars ever. I asked my dad for one last year, and he told me to get real. Instead, I needed something cute and durable. Men are so chauvinistic." For some reason, Tony found that to be funny. "It's not funny. I like muscle cars, so why can't a girl have one if a boy can? Everybody knows women are better drivers anyway," I said, all riled up.

"I'm not about to debate sexism with you, or we will be here all night. I believe in equal rights, so you can take that up with your dad," Tony said, half looking at the road and me.

"Fine, what's up with the change of plans? Or are we bailing on my friends because if so, I am not okay with that and..."

He cut me off, telling me to calm down and take a breather. "One day I will let you drive the car, okay. I can respect any woman who can appreciate a nice car."

Flattered he called me a woman, I had to conceal a smile. "Good, so then I can show you how this puppy really handles. Like I said, women are better drivers. We can multitask. Sorry, I got excited," I apologized, but chauvinism irks me. "What is with the change of plans and the secrecy in the lot?"

"It's cool. I set the meeting back an hour, remembering the step competition today. I knew how badly you wanted to go. That way you could hang with your friends a bit, so the meeting is at midnight now. I just needed to catch up with you to let you know. As far as hushing you in the lot, we have to be extra careful in case anyone, like that punk, is watching or listening to us," Tony said, sounding still angry that the boy stepped to me and not him.

Men and their egos. I handled myself quite well, but he was right. "I understand, especially since we know there is someone else who knows about us but we don't know a thing about him. Thank you for thinking of me. What did the others say when you told them?" I asked.

"Don't worry about them, they always set the time. I explained the situation, and they understood. I really didn't care if they didn't like it," he said.

"Afterward, we will come up with some excuse to leave, then I will take you home after. Is that okay?" he asked.

"Works for me, and thank you, Tony, that was really sweet of you."

We drove the rest of the way, making small talk and rehashing the competition. We finally arrived at the burger joint just in time because my stomach was about to eat itself. Some people were already there ordering, and some just got there when we did.

We ordered, we grubbed, we laughed, then Tony and I bounced. I was glad because the "I told you so" looks I kept getting from the Angela and Hope drove me nuts.

He took his time driving while we talked and acted silly from the drunkenness of good food. His sense of humor was somewhat goofy like mine, so the conversation flowed. As soon as we arrived, all we wanted was a nap, but tonight's meeting was important.

Chapter 13

Like last time, we were the last ones to arrive, and of course, the others dressed as if they stepped out of a fashion magazine. Let them have fashion; I like my geeky gear.

"Nice of you two to show up," Cheyenne said as soon as we entered the room before we could even take a seat. She sat in the black chair facing the entry with her arms delicately displayed on the armrest of the chair, her body stiffly positioned, showing no emotion.

Rolling my eyes and sighing, I sat as far away as possible from her. Okay, I got the hint; there was definitely something between the two of them. Whatever it was, that was for him to handle, not me.

"Sorry, we got here as soon as we could. Anything new?" Tony said, ignoring her cold stare; he sat down on the couch, away from her.

Willow spoke up first. "Byron may have stumbled upon something new," she said it trying to sound bubbly, but I detected a hint of sadness in her voice that she tried to hide, but it piqued my curiosity as to why wouldn't she be overjoyed with the possibility of new information.

"Yeah, I visited my grandfather recently and managed to get some alone time with him since he has help around him all the time. I tried asking him about me and the possibility of me being different," Byron said.

"See, he had always been the head of my family. He was heavily involved in the finances and our livelihood. Why? Probably because when he was young, he invested in some private organization and made bank. Other than that, I do not know. All I know is my dad allowed it even when they argued," Byron explained.

Willow jumped up, sounding all too perky this time. "Mr. Conway, Byron's grandfather is loaded. My family is rich, but he is richer than God is. This man ran every business in town. People practically bowed down…"

Byron grabbed her arm. "Okay, Willow, I think they got it." He sounded a little embarrassed.

"Sorry, I got a little carried away," she said, then sat back down, still smiling from ear to ear. She reminds me of those future homemakers that only cared about the money and status.

My mom has to deal with some of those women who come in to volunteer at the clinic, complaining about what a hard life they have because they have to drive a year-old car or their husbands have to work long hours—usually something trivial—while the patients that come in are sick, poor, and/or can barely buy food, among a million other problems. Greediness and snobs really piss me off. Just because you're well-off doesn't mean you should flaunt or brag about it.

Realizing I was staring at Willow and not Byron, who was talking, I pushed her out my mind to listen.

"Anyway, he was mumbling on about some hidden organization that no one really fully comprehended but him. I asked him what he meant, but he has dementia, memory loss, so it was vague, and you can't always get straight answers out of him. Some days he is lucid, and other days he's not." As Byron continued, he kept fidgeting with his glasses. I got the impression he didn't like talking too much about private affairs.

"He told me we should have never brought that evil into the family. He got all upset with me, saying I should have been stronger than he was. Then kept shouting 'Evil is among us all and my soul is forsaken' repeatedly. He got so upset, he had a seizure. Before I could calm him down, the nurse, along with Hanna, the headmistress, did something to calm him down, got scolded by Hanna, and then they took him upstairs to rest. I have never seen him act like that. In this past year, he has gotten considerably worse," Byron said.

"I'm sorry about your grandfather, but why would he say that to you?" I asked.

"He sometimes confuses me with my father, so maybe he thought he was talking to my dad." For the fifth time, he removed his glasses to wipe them clean again. I wanted to tell him to stop or there wouldn't be any glass left.

"Anyway, I remembered my dad packing up some of my grandfather's files and other important papers last year and storing them in the basement of the west wing. For the past three months, my dad has been visiting him a lot more," he said, emphasizing the words "a lot."

126

"Is that unusual for your dad to visit him? If he was involved in the finances, maybe your dad has been picking his brain for some new money-making deal. I mean, when he is lucid," Tony asked.

"Maybe he was not so much visiting him but researching something," Byron said.

"Research what? Let's go to your grandfather's house and find out," I said louder than expected from sheer excitement of this discovery; finally, a break.

"I don't know what exactly, but I was thinking about us going there too," Byron said, looking in Willow's direction, the latter part of his sentence trailing off.

"I mean now," I said. "Look, we are all together now, and there is no better time than the present. I just developed this, whatever you want to call it, and I'm very interested in finding out as much as possible." It was so silent in the room, you could hear a pin drop. My heart sank. Was no one was up for this?

"What's up with you, guys? Byron, when you spoke, you kept cleaning your glasses as if you were wiping the filth off, as in yours. Are you guys ashamed to be different or something?" I asked.

"Listen, Connor, not all of us was gung ho as you when we discovered our abilities," said Cheyenne. "People look up to us."

I was trying my best to ignore her, and it was getting harder and harder to do. She really worked my last nerve.

"Yeah, Cheyenne, Byron, and I come from pretty wealthy families, you know," Willow said.

"So? I'm not impressed. What's your point?" I asked. "These abilities are more of a burden to us. We live in

a cookie-cutter world where if you are different, you get shunned," Willow explained. "I'm not trying to sound like a snob, but it's just the way things are."

I stood up, walked behind the couch, took some deep breaths, then counted to ten. I stayed behind the couch facing the others, trying not to lose it. "Are you kidding me? So what are you saying? You don't want to know what is going on? Because I sure do. I want to know how we came to be and what he meant by 'evil.'"

"Probably nothing, Connor, the man has dementia," Tony said. "Sorry, Byron." Byron nodded in his direction as if to say, "It's cool." "I agree with Connor—"

"Of course you do," Cheyenne said, cutting him off.

Tony let out a long sigh. "Like I was saying, I agree with Connor." He stared directly at Cheyenne, giving her the "back off" glare. "We need to know more. I have been sitting back on this because you all have been hesitant. Now we may possibly have a lead, so let's follow up on it."

"Why are you guys pushing this so hard?" asked Willow. "What gives?"

Tony and I told them about the boy from school and the fight. By the time we finished, everybody was up out of their seats, talking at once.

"Why are you just now telling us this? That should have been the first thing out of your mouth tonight," Byron said, clearly upset. "You could have at least called me, Tony."

"Sorry. I should have let you know, and tonight when you started talking, it slipped my mind," Tony said.

"Are you okay? Who is this boy?" Byron asked me.

"I have only seen him once at school before but never saw him glow before only that one time," I explained.

"I want to meet this kid and find out who he is," Tony said to Byron who nodded. "He could expose us."

"We definitely have to talk to him. I say we all meet at your school Monday, seek him out, then approach him after school. Agreed?" Byron asked.

"Sounds like a plan," Tony agreed along with the rest of us.

I thought, finally a plan to get things done. "Anyway, now do you see why we need to find out what is going on ASAP?" I said.

"What is going on? This is not good at all. This is getting way too deep," Willow whined.

What did she think was going to happen, this would go away if she ignored things long enough?

"It's okay, Willow, don't stress. You don't have to do anything you don't want to," Byron said, trying to console her as she fell into his arms.

Just when Byron took a step forward, she pulled him two steps back. I'm sure Willow was a very nice girl, but she started getting on my nerves too. They all did at this point. Even Tony pacified them too much for me.

I told myself, "Connor, be nice," but my little self-pep talk didn't exactly work because words were spewing out my mouth, filter off. I pretty much told them all what I thought about their stall tactics, about selfish people, and how they hold others back. They didn't like it, but unbeknownst to them, they don't get to run me. I was on a mission, so either join me or move out of my way.

"So are you going to give me the keys to your grandfather's house, Byron, or do I have to break in? Heads up, if I get caught, I'm naming names," I said, pointed to each one of them. "We poor folk in noncookie-cutter worlds have no standards, so let's be real, me breaking into a house to find answers are acceptable, right?" I acted so obnoxiously animated as the words came out my mouth, but I didn't care.

"I hate to break it to you, but this is not going away, Willow. Our cover is blown, so it's time to face reality, people, because you don't have a choice." I don't know what came over me, but I needed answers, and I was going to get them one way or another. Besides, they're not the ones getting in fights and sensing someone following them.

Willow and Byron stood there with their mouths open, Cheyenne had the "if the looks could kill expression" targeted at me most likely, plotting my death, while Tony stared me down.

"Remind me never to piss you off, but she is right, guys. I have sat back and let you run the show, but no more. I'm with you, Connor," Tony said, standing by my side.

"Fine, then we can go, but why can't we wait until daylight like civilized people?" Willow asked.

She made me want to vomit from the naïveté of it all. "Oh yes, I can see it now. While we are having tea and crumpets, we will simply ask, 'So, Gramps, what exactly did you mean when you said 'evil'?"

Cheyenne turned her head, stifling a laugh. If she found this amusing, why didn't she speak up or back me up? I was past hot at this point.

"There is no way I will allow any of you to stop me from…"

Suddenly, Tony grabbed me, saying something, but I ignored him. I finally shut up when a chair flew my way, forcing me to the floor.

"Damn, your eyes are glowing. They're…," Tony said. "Violet," Willow cut in, standing over me.

"You're going to have to learn to control that temper if this is what happens," Tony said to me as I got up.

Willow shoved a mirror in my face, and sure enough, my eyes were glowing violet. It was wicked.

Before I could ask if they had experienced this, they were huddled around me. I hit Byron's hands a couple of times when he tried to touch my eyes. Eventually, they returned to their normal shade of brown.

Byron shook his head, mouth open. "No, you're the only one, Connor. And by the way, this is you?" he asked, pointing to the furniture.

The room was in disarray of scattered furniture and torn curtains. "Sorry." What else could I say?

On that note, we decided not to wait any longer and head to Byron's grandfather's house that night.

Chapter 14

We climbed into Byron's Range Rover toward their neighborhood. It was about a thirty-minute drive, riding mostly in silence, probably stressed about what to expect. I was thinking about wanting to find answers, Willow about not wanting to find answers, Byron about something rational, Tony about something irrational, and Cheyenne probably about which animal she should kill next.

We took a winding road near the cliff by the shore. The road was wide enough for another car to pass, but it seemed for a Friday night, hardly anyone was out or most likely headed toward the city.

We reached the border of their town, and already I could see the homes driving in, and they were amazing. Willow was not exaggerating about where they came from. The homes were extravagant.

Most were set back behind gated fences with armed guards or coded keypads. It was right out of fashion magazines Angela, Hope, and I read, hoping to own ourselves one day. It made my neighborhood look frumpy.

Okay, so I get some of what she was saying. I probably couldn't even begin to comprehend the pressures they have to put up with, but they are still just like Tony and me, and that is what we came here to find out—how.

We finally arrived at his grandfather's home, and his too was behind a gated fence but with a keypad for access and a booth for a guard, but that sat empty. Not sure if that was luck or not, but I will take it.

"Hey, Byron, aren't they going to know the gate has opened?" I asked.

"Yes, but I sometimes crash here, so Hanna won't think anything of it. I will park in the garage behind the house, then sneak you inside so if you see any staff members, please hide as quickly as possible. They do roam at night for whatever reason."

Byron punched in a code, and the gate opened up for us. As we drove up, we passed tall sculptures surrounded by flowers that I have never seen before, unlike your typical roses. There was a bench next to a bridge crossing over a small pond. There were topiary shrubs and hedges in many different shapes and sizes. There were high statues elegantly placed, and I can only imagine hidden paths in the gardens that I would love to explore.

When his house came more visible, it was more like a grand castle than a house. It was made of gray stone, with bricks strategically placed in the center of each corner. Huge stained-glass windows were used along the top floor. Green vines covered the corners in the front of the castle. I felt like we went back into time.

There was even a water fountain in the middle of the cobblestone driveway about fifty feet from the front door. This place was stunning. If I were not here to see it myself, I would not believe it. I had to wonder, even if I had all the money in the world, why on earth would I need a place this big?

We turned left, passing the castle, a clearing, then turned right, meeting up to a path that led us along high bushes to our left. We followed the path into complete darkness other than the car headlights.

Eventually, we drove into a five-car garage and parked. Byron handed us each flashlights from a box on a shelf in case we needed them, then we headed toward the back door.

Not able to get into the main house through the back garage, we had to walk outside to reach the main house. There wasn't much lighting from the house, and the woods were behind us. I was just hoping no one would catch us.

Chapter 15

We followed Byron inside, walking as quietly possible, down a hallway passing a little room to the left that appeared to be a break room.

We kept going straight until it eventually opened up into a large sitting area to the left. The room decorated conservatively with tall plants in each corner, old paintings of stuffy-looking men, other small furnishings, and naked statues. It reminded me of a museum.

On the right of us were two huge cherry-wood doors with little round windows big enough to look through. Not able to help myself, I peeped through each. Each door encased a kitchen, one larger than the other was.

I cracked the door to the second kitchen to see that it was huge, with cherry-wood paneling that had silver and black as the primary colors. There were so many silver cooking utensils, six wooden islands to prepare food on, five black stoves to cook, and four huge silver sinks to clean. Oh my goodness, what a feast this place could dream up.

Not paying attention, someone covered my mouth, grabbed me, and dragged me behind a secluded statue in the corner. It was Tony manhandling me.

I tried to free myself until I heard someone coming. I could see through the statue's arm it was a young woman carrying a silver tray with a used, milky glass and a half-eaten sandwich on a plate. She was probably carrying someone's midnight snack.

When she passed by and went into the smaller kitchen, Tony uncovered my mouth, and we both took a breath. We were in such a small spot, he pressed up against me. We didn't move while we were waiting for her to leave.

It started to get claustrophobic in such a tight spot. Couldn't he have found a bigger one? Please, lady, would you hurry up? I closed my eyes and took some deep breaths, trying to relax, but all I could focus on was Tony's scent. He always smelled good.

I felt his heart beating erratically fast, so I opened my eyes to see if he was okay, only to find him staring at me. He just kept staring, not saying anything. It started to feel warm, a little too warm, in that tiny space we barely fit. He started squeezing my arms tightly, I couldn't move. I went from barely breathing to breathing hard. The heat that was rising off us was almost unbearable, but he wouldn't let me move.

His eyes, his eyes glowed yellow. Is that what I looked like?

"Tony..." was the only sound that escaped me before he left me standing there. What was that? I heard about raging teen hormones, but that seemed more like crazy teen hormones. Why did his eyes...

"Come on," Cheyenne said, watching me. "What is wrong with you? Are you trying to get us caught?" She was whispering, but it came across more as a hiss.

"No, let's go," I said, waving for her to proceed. She looked like she wanted to say something at first but thought better of it and walked off.

Trying to keep up with her long-legged strides, I had to ask, "What's your problem?" Big mistake, I regretted it as soon as it came out, not what I said, only the time and place.

She swung around so fast I had to catch myself, so as not to slam into her. "I'm so sick and tired of your innocent naïve act, making sure Tony has to pine all over you."

"You jealous little witch. He doesn't pine over me. It's not my fault he doesn't want…"

"You stupid, stupid girl, don't be so simple. I don't want him because if I did, he would be mine. We are good friends, so it is my job to protect him from girls like you. You play all innocent, but something about you I don't trust…" Cheyenne snapped.

"You must have me confused with yourself because you know nothing about me, and this little tough act you got going on doesn't scare me one bit, so don't think for one second I won't take you on. You can lie to yourself all you want, but it's obvious you're pining away for him."

"What is going on out here?" Byron stepped out of the dark. "This is supposed to be a secret mission, remember, not girls gone wild. You two are going to wake everybody up."

Willow showed up soon after Byron did and gave Cheyenne a look, then put her hands on her hips. I had a feeling she knew exactly what was going on.

"Let's go," Byron said walking off, he made a right just past the sitting room, turning on his flashlight, and we followed suit. He led us down a flight of stairs winding left, ending at another long dark hallway so Byron turned on the lights making it extremely bright.

The walls were canary yellow and covered with old paintings. We passed several smaller sitting rooms similar to upstairs. The hallway went on forever, passing door after door until we saw a lit room off to the left, which was the last room of the hall. Stacked boxes and old furniture filled the room.

Tony was in the back of the room, moving boxes, and glanced at the rest of us, confused. His glare stopped in Cheyenne's direction, and he didn't look pleased.

I couldn't believe I was baited into an argument over a guy. I hate girls who fight over guys, but there was no way I will let Cheyenne think she can walk all over me.

As soon as the guys started moving the boxes in front of a door we needed to get to, I told them to step aside and let me do it. I moved the boxes that were blocking the door, then stepped back. I set on doing this and getting out of here. It is amazing what you can do with a focused mind.

Byron turned on the lights and yes, you guessed it—it was a dark, dank room, filled with numerous green-and-black metal filing cabinets along the walls and stacks of papers in the middle of the room on two wooden desks.

The room was unnecessarily huge, covered with pale white walls without windows, puke-green tiled floor, and as luck would have it, no chairs. At least the temperature down here was all right.

"Well, I don't really know where to begin, guys, so start anywhere," Byron suggested.

No one said a word as we set off in opposite directions. I went to the far left until I came upon a big black filing cabinet that was open and got to work.

It seemed like we were there for hours, searching for something, praying for anything. By now, everyone had gotten comfortable by sitting either on the floor or by leaning against cabinets with shoes off. I wondered if they were feeling hopeless like me but refused to ask.

Finally, someone spoke up, and surprisingly it was Willow. "I think I found something." Everyone dropped what they were doing and ran over to her, asking questions at once.

Her bubbly demeanor quickly turned distressing. "It says something about Byron being adopted from a place called the Caring House." She handed Byron a green folder.

"Let me see that. I'm adopted?" He took the papers from Willow to look them over.

"Well, actually if you think about it, it fits with what your grandfather said to you, thinking you were your dad. Remember 'bringing evil into this family'? Maybe he meant you were the evil your father brought in through adoption," Tony said.

Byron gave Tony a look like "really, man." "Yes, thanks for reminding me because I almost forgot."

We all, except Byron, dug in that general area until we found folders on each of us and one other. It seems as if adoption was the case for the rest of us as well.

Inside was a copy of certificates of adoption sixteen years ago, all from this place called the Caring House. On the top of each certificate were the same six names, names we had never heard of or seen before, with each of our parents' signatures.

Most of the paperwork in the folders was written in this bizarre handwriting we didn't understand, maybe some kind of shorthand. We couldn't read any of the other pages because we simply couldn't figure out what type of script it was. It was the strangest thing I had ever seen.

"This doesn't make any sense. I wasn't born yet. How could I have been at this place?" I asked no one in particular, not wanting to believe.

"Maybe it's not right, you know, inaccurate. My parents couldn't have adopted me sixteen years ago. This is not real," Willow said, tossing her folder in the air.

"Think about it, Willow. You always said that you felt different from your family, and believe me, I can relate," Cheyenne said, bending down to pick up the papers Willow tossed. I was shocked.

"Me too," Tony said.

"No, I don't believe it. What's the chances of us all getting adopted at the same time, and why does your grandfather have these folders on us and others anyway, Byron?" Willow's whole body was trembling as she spoke calmly, almost too calmly. "Oh my god, your grandfather has so much power and control over everything, it's frightening. Is it because he made a deal with the devil, or is he the devil himself? Which is it, Byron?" she shouted at him.

You could hear the electricity build up inside of her. We all slowly stepped back from her, but when her hands went up, we barely had time to get out of the way before electricity shot across the room.

We hid behind cabinets, yelling for her to calm down. Metal, not a good place for hiding, but our options were limited.

I tried keeping the bolts from hitting anyone by diverting them to the walls, but I was not able to catch them all. A couple of cabinets flew into walls, and some papers caught fire. This was a disaster. How is no one upstairs hearing this?

Byron caught my attention and nodded toward Willow. He, being the quickest, was going

147

to try to get to her. So if I missed diverting a bolt, he can get out of dodge quickly.

He ran over, tackled her, and eventually calmed her down. Whatever he said must have worked because there were no more lightning bolts.

Once the coast was clear, we walked over to them. Byron was telling Willow, "I'm sorry, but we all agreed,

no matter what, we would accept the answers we find. We are all in this together. You are not alone, and right now nothing has to change."

"Yes, it does. I'm sorry, Willow, but we can't stop here. I need to know more about my real family. I need to know more now that we found these folders," Cheyenne said.

"Right, and what about that boy who attacked Connor in school? According to the last folder, his name could be Scott Dasher, but who's to say your grandfather has all the folders? There could be others," Tony said.

I was about to add to what Tony said, but something caught my attention. There was a folder on the floor next to me titled the Deckers. It must have flown out of the cabinet Willow struck.

I grabbed it up, hoping I was wrong. Flipping through the pages, my worst fears came true Angela Decker, my best friend's family, was somehow involved, but how?

There were pages of that stupid gibberish I couldn't make out, but upon flipping through it, I found another certificate of adoption. It was not Angela's name but Vincent, her adopted brother who went missing twelve years ago. He was four when he disappeared.

Oh no, do my parents know about me? Will the rest of us go missing too? Does Angela know about me? It could explain why she needs to know everything I do.

"What, Connor, what?" Byron asked.

I explained what I found, who Vincent was, and how nobody knows what happened to him. Angela searches for his name every so often, but it's like he vanished.

"Connor may be right because lately I had a strong feeling I'm being followed," Cheyenne said.

"Me too," I confessed. "I don't mean the boy from school but everywhere, and for a long time now."

"Are we the only ones?" Cheyenne asked. Byron admitted he has felt it too, but Tony and Willow said they haven't noticed.

We all agreed it was time to go. Now feeling rushed, we agreed to make some calls regarding the Caring House and, next weekend, no matter what, go visit it.

Byron reassured us that the basement was soundproof, and a war could have erupted and no one upstairs would have heard a thing. He said he would come back tomorrow early with helpers to clean up.

The ride back home was quiet. We came here for answers and ended up with more questions than before.

Sneaking back into my house, I noticed Mrs. Palmer had her lights on. I don't think that woman ever slept. She had company, but who knows, it could be her husband since you never see him. He supposedly works for some huge company overseas and comes home twice a month. I never really paid them much attention.

By the time I snuck back in and climbed into bed, it was 4:00 a.m. Even as exhausted as I was, I couldn't help wonder about the unanswered questions, and what did Byron's grandfather have to do with this?

Most of all, I'm adopted.

Chapter 16

The next morning, I woke to the raised voices of my parents. They were fussing right outside my door.

Oh crap, they must have known I snuck in last night. How? I was quiet. No way or they would have either been waiting in my room or barged in as I crawled through the window.

I slowly got up to open the door and face my sentence. I tried to come up with a good excuse before they confronted me, but when I opened the door, no one was there. I peeked down the hall and in the other rooms, but didn't find them there either. That is strange.

I grabbed my cell heading downstairs and found them out back on the patio. From the hallway next to the stairs, I watched them through the back door window. Whew, they were fussing about Ebony staying out late and lying about it. About time. Crisis averted.

"Connor, when did you get up? How long were you standing there?" My mom said, swinging open the door after shushing my dad.

"Oh, not long, I just woke up. So what's going on?" I asked, busted for eavesdropping.

"Nothing, sweetie, you must have been tired. It's almost twelve already," she said with the fakest grin I had ever seen cross her face.

"School, school, school. Study, study, study," I said, all goofy like, not doing any better than my mom at hiding a lie.

"You want lunch or something?" she asked.

Why is she being nice to me? "No. Remember, Angie and I have plans to do the shopping-and-movie thing today?"

"You need some money, honey?" my dad asked. Okay, something is seriously up because my dad never offers money, ever. I must be dying, or maybe they feel guilty for working me like a slave around here while Ebony never helped.

"Ummmm, sure, Dad, I do need some new jeans." Hey, why not take advantage of it? If I'm going out, I may as well go out looking good.

"Okay, I will put some money on the kitchen counter by the phone."

"Thanks, Dad," I said, walking off quickly, hoping he would not realize what he said and change his mind.

Halfway down the hall, I stopped cold and dropped my phone. I heard my parents all the way from the other side of the house, just as clear as they were right in front of me.

Is it possible that I could have a third ability? I have the ability of invisibility, telekinesis, and now enhanced hearing.

I listened for the birds singing outside, the bees humming in the flowers, the water drip from the faucet in the upstairs bathroom, and the trees blowing in the wind. It was surreal. It felt as if I was next to each one, so I closed my eyes and pretended I was. It felt like heaven, all warm and cozy.

"What are you smiling about, alien head?" Kane said, standing there in is his red cape, water gun aimed at me.

Oh great, Reptile Boy. I thought we set him free in the woods. Drat, he must have found his way back. Trying to ignore him and find my way back to heaven, he sprayed me in the face with water, so my inner child kicked in and joined in the water fight.

We ran around the whole house, me with cups, and he had the super-duper soaker gun, screaming and jumping, having fun. I broke a mug—who cares I'll clean that later—and kept on going. Even our little Jack Russell was chiming in, barking, and bouncing off the furniture.

I was drenched from my head to my toes and loved every minute of it. I guess that at times my little brother could be fun. Last night felt like a distant memory, and that is how I want to keep it, distant for as long as I can.

After what seemed like hours of fun, the doorbell rang. The living room clock read one o'clock, but Angie wasn't supposed to be here until two or, as in her case, three.

Expecting to see Angela's face explaining why she came so early, I swung open the front door, but as fate would have it, Tony stood in my doorway.

He checked me from head to toe, eyeing me curiously. "Hey, Sci-fi, you just stepped out the shower?"

I'm supposed to be annoyed with him, but I was over it. That was yesterday's news, and I'm a woman of today. Where do I come up with this stuff?

"Who's there?" My dad came up behind me, being nosy. "Hey, son, we're not buying anything," he said, and he tried closing the door in Tony's face.

"Dad!" I squealed, grabbing the door. He can be so rude sometimes.

"Stop it, Blair, they probably know each other," my mom said, trying to save me from my dad's eternal embarrassment. "Come in. Connor, let the young man in." But she was smiling as if it was prom night or something. Now who is going to save me from her?

"Hello, Mr. and Mrs. Esquibel. I'm Tony. Connor and I go to school together."

"Nice to meet you, Tony," my mom politely said, turning to my dad who wasn't so nice. "Blair."

My dad stood there, arms folded, eyeing Tony suspiciously, and made a noise of the nonhuman kind. Did he really just grunt? My dad seriously grunted at him.

"We're going to the patio." I grabbed Tony's arm, walking off toward the back but would have preferred to drop into a black hole, which is quicker to get to, and the furthest away.

"Sure, dear," my mom said right before asking, "Who broke a glass in the kitchen and left it?"

"Reptile Boy," I yelled back and hurried up.

Making it to the patio in record time, I asked him to have a seat, but he refused and leaned against the railing instead, so I did the same. I apologized for my dad's behavior, explaining it was probably some old people mental disorder disease. "So what's up?" I asked, wondering what prompted this unexpected visit.

"Let's go," he said with no further explanation. "What? Where?"

"The Caring House, today."

"I thought we were going to make some calls regarding this place, check out its history, form a plan before we head out there blind," I said.

"I know, but I was thinking if we call ahead then we give people heads up, and I don't want to do that. We have waited long enough, and I'm ready for some answers. Aren't you?" he asked.

"What people, Tony? You act like there is some big conspiracy or something."

"No, I'm just saying I don't want to give people a heads up. After what you said about Vincent last night and people following you, Byron, and Cheyenne, I think we should act now. You know you're taking this adoption thing in stride. I'm a wreck. I hardly slept last night. I wanted come here five hours ago. What's your secret?"

"I don't know why I'm not more upset, honestly, maybe because I woke up in my bed in my room to the sound of my parents' voices. So to me, nothing has changed, or it just hasn't hit me yet."

"It's called denial, Connor, and we need to face it and fast."

"Before all this started, I already had a superpower, which gives me the ability to ignore, suppress, or categorize my emotions. And if that's what I need to do right now to function, then so be it."

He looked so tired, this obviously was bothering him a lot, as it should, so why wasn't I more upset? He was right about one thing, I do need to face reality and exit stage right of fantasyland.

"Yeah, it's called denial."

"Whatever, did you call the others yet?" I asked. "No, I came straight here," he said.

"Oh, I figured you would have gone straight to Cheyenne." Did that just slip out my mouth?

That comment got me a cold stare and a long sigh before a response. "Why would you say that?"

"Well, to hear her tell it, if she wanted to, she could have you at any time. I thought you two had a thing from the first time I met her," I said.

"Oh really, and that's not true. We were the first to meet, and thinking that we were the only ones made us close. Besides, she has and always had a boyfriend, as far as I can remember," he said.

"So what did you do to lead her on?" I asked.

"I never led her on, so get that right out of your head. We did a lot of talking and always joked one day we would save the world together, that kind of corny stuff. Please, she would drop me like a hot potato whenever her boyfriend called," he said.

"She doesn't like me like that, Connor, honest. She's the overprotective type," he explained.

He caught me off guard when he stepped close to me, so I backed up a little. "I'm drawn to you, Connor. Come on, I show up at your house in the middle of the night. I think about you all the time and have even spoken to Cheyenne about it. At first she seemed cool with it, but now all of a sudden, she's upset about it."

Boys are so clueless. Of course, she's going to play it off. No wonder she hates me. She probably wanted him to wait around for her in case she broke things off with her boyfriend.

"Maybe she genuinely likes you, have you ever thought about that? Besides, she's pretty, rich, and has legs for miles. Who wouldn't want her?" I said, folding my arms, trying to act as if I could care less if he went to her as I closely watched his reaction to my comment.

"That's your opinion. You're the beauty. I'm crazy about your wild curly hair, your personality, and I don't think you heard me say that I am drawn to you." He stepped in close to me again and started touching my hair, but this time, I didn't move back. I swallowed hard. I missed the part about being drawn to me. The butterflies in my stomach stirred.

His eyes turned from light brown to yellow right in front of me, but before I could say anything, he kissed me, and I kissed back. He pressed my back against the house, holding me tightly like before, grabbing my hair, and kissing me fiercely, making the butterflies flutter wildly.

"Um, hello." I heard a female's voice behind Tony.

I broke from Tony, who must not have heard her, because at first he appeared startled. I was patting my hair back down, eyeing Angie who had the biggest grin ever, eyeing me from the bottom of the steps, wearing the latest fashion. Of all people to show up, why I am not surprised it's her? She lives for the latest gossip.

"I have heard of raging teenage hormones before, but that kiss made me want to blush. It was like in the movies or those Spanish soap operas. Girl, if I hadn't shown up, who knows what would have happened next. I'm jealous." As she walked up with patio steps, she was putting emphasis on each word.

"Just friends, my butt, you little sneak. I knew there was more between the two of you. I wish

Bobby kissed me like that," Angie said, now not five feet from me, making me feel uncomfortable.

Tony walked to the other side of the patio covered by shade in order to calm himself so his eyes could revert. I'm lucky mine didn't do anything crazy. Angie was always popping up at the wrong times.

"Hey, Angie. You're a little early, aren't you?" I sounded out of breath but tried to play if off.

"I know, but I needed to get out of the house. My mom was driving me crazy with chores," she said.

"Hey, Tony. I don't need to ask how you are doing. Seems to me you are doing just fine." She was trying to get a reaction out of him, but he didn't bite. He kept his distance on the other side of the porch, facing us, not saying a word.

"Really, Angie," I said, cutting her a look to stop. "Fine, how about we go shopping another day? I would

feel so guilty separating you two. Besides, Bobby asked me to go out anyway. I told him no, but I can certainly call him back."

"No, Angie, we can go shopping. It's no problem." "No, do you, because I want to hear all the gossip later,"

she whispered.

"It is not like that, Angie," I said. She doesn't know when to let up ever. She is so full of it. She's never done anything with a boy either. Bobby is a straight-up science geek and an undercover *Star Wars* lover.

"Actually, that will work, Angie, thanks. I just asked Connor to take a ride with me." Tony walked over, his voice deeper than I had ever heard before, his expression serious, arms folded, and he leaned against the pole. His eyes were back to normal, but his mood wasn't.

"No problem, Tony. We have to double date soon. Kisses," she said, running off, giggling.

This would be on the Internet as soon as she got in the car. "Tony, I had plans, you know," I said, sounding a little annoyed with what just happened.

He didn't say a word, only stared at me. I got the hint he was not backing down.

"Fine, give me thirty minutes, okay?" I said. "Fifteen."

He still had a look about him that meant business, so I reserved my sarcastic comment and was ready in twenty. I never showered so fast in my life.

Chapter 17

About twenty-two minutes and a little lie later, we were on the road. Not that I like lying to my parents, but this was important.

"So what's the plan?" I asked.

"There isn't one. We're winging it. We go there and see what we can find out."

"You're the boss." Not that I thought this would work, but he seemed to be on a mission, and hey, you never know.

We drove mostly in silence not by my choice, but Tony seemed to be in a crazy serious mood, so I let him be. I kept drifting back to the kiss and those butterflies would flare up again. I've never been kissed like that in my life. Trying to ignore the wildlife in my stomach, I allowed myself a midafternoon nap.

Tony woke me up as we drove into a nice peaceful town that looked like a small local tourist attraction. According to the phone's GPS, it should have taken a normal driver ninety minutes to get here, but with Tony's driving, we made it in seventy.

We passed modest-looking homes, a couple of public schools with two nice-sized playgrounds, and a few grocery stores. There were boutiques along what seemed to be the main strip of the town. People were coming in and out of shops with bags of recent buys. Kids were everywhere: some eating ice cream on benches, some in strollers, or running rampant. It seemed like a cozy place to live.

The town park was hosting some kind of fair, so we decided to go check it out first. We parked in a nearby lot, hoping to fit in with the locals, then decided to walk from here. The Caring House was only a few blocks away.

I felt the heat as soon as I opened the door and it was blazing hot. Getting out the car to stretch, I asked, "How come you don't always drive to the meetings late at night?" "I don't want my dad to hear the car drive off and get busted," he said, then asked, "Are you hungry?" I gave him an enthusiastic yes without shame. Between playing with Kane and Tony popping up, I hadn't thought about food.

We grabbed some grub, found a table, and after finishing off two hot dogs, a slice of NY-style pizza, two scoops of ice cream including the cone, and a big cup of soda, Tony couldn't help but be amazed. My belly was full, and I was content.

"What? I was hungry!" Am I to feel embarrassment because I have a healthy appetite, which seems to get healthier by the minute?

"I could tell. You didn't come up for air once. You are definitely not a cheap date," he said, edging back as if I were going to gobble him up too.

I punched him in the arm. "Ha-ha, if this were a date, my friend, you would not be feeding me hot dogs and ice cream. Not that you can talk, you didn't do too shabby yourself, buddy." We cracked jokes on each other for a while, and before long, we were back to normal.

After we ate, we decided to head toward the Caring House, which was only two blocks away. We approached a two-story wooden house with a sign on the front lawn that said "The Caring House: a home away from home."

It was a pretty mint-green two-story house with white shutters. Green grass spread across the front yard that was tidy and well kept. Off to the left of the house, there were two station wagons parked in the driveway in front of a two-door garage that was the same color as the house. The porch extended around the sides of the house, decorated with white wicker couches, chairs, and colorful cushions filled their seats. It looked so very much like a Barbie doll's house that it almost didn't look real.

As pretty as this place appeared to be, it gave me the creeps, but I shook it off for the sake of the mission. "Okay, now that we're here, what's the brilliant plan?" I asked.

"We want to know more about us. Maybe they can lead us to someone who can help, and if that doesn't work, we will distract whoever and break into the records," Tony said, walking up the walkway, not breaking stride, as if breaking into a house was the norm.

"Wait, what? Are you crazy? We could get caught breaking in. You never said anything about breaking in," I said.

"Listen, we didn't come here for tea and crumpets. Well, at least I didn't," he said, taking the steps by twos.

"I don't appreciate you throwing my words back at me. That was a different situation, and you know it." He rang the bell, not responding to my last statement, and refused to look at me. He had a goal in mind but forgot to clue me in on all the plans. What did I just get myself into?

A minute later, a woman about sixty opened the main door but kept the screen shut. She seemed a bit put off by us from her tone. Her face scrunched up as if she just ate a rotten piece of candy or she didn't like daylight. She wore purple horn-rimmed glasses, and her dark hair stood pinned up in a bun on her head so tightly, it had to hurt. She dressed as if style was unknown to her in an old-fashioned white-laced, long-sleeved shirt and a long blue skirt with black boots. Did she not get the memo that it's warm out?

"Yes, may I help you?" she asked, holding on to her glasses.

"Hello, my name is Tony, and this is Connor. Years ago we were adopted from here, and now we are searching for more information on our parents."

All right now, don't hold back any. Just let it all hang out, buddy. Was he purposely botching this so we would have to break in?

"Well, if neither one of you is eighteen, and you certainly don't look it, or older, then I simply cannot help you. Ask your adopted parents to file the appropriate papers, and the state will follow up," she said, sounding every bit the rude person I expected her to be.

"Ethel, who is at the door?" An older woman appeared at the door with a smile. Maybe we have a chance after all. She was short, stocky, and wore a plain blue dress. It seemed to suit her somehow. She, unlike Ethel, seemed delighted to see us.

"They wanted some information on their adoptions, so I was explaining to them we simply cannot help," the woman named Ethel answered.

"Oh, Ethel. Come on in, kids, and have a seat. Surely we can invite them in," the older woman said, opening the screen door for us to enter.

"Marge, you will take in anyone. Well, you deal with them. I have some paperwork to do," Ethel said, walking off.

"Don't mind her, kids, she has been a little stressed lately. Anyway, come in and have a seat in my office. I am Ms. Ridgemont."

We followed her down a long hallway lined with shiny dark wood paneling, passing a small hall on the left, but I couldn't see where it led. On the right, there were double doors that opened to a sitting area, and right past the doorway to the left, along the wall, was a stairwell leading up.

As we followed, we each tried to take in the lay of the land. I felt like I was casing the joint for a bank robbery. She stopped at an old cluttered office, stacked high with papers that needed a lot of attending to.

"Have a seat. Now how can I help you two lovelies?" she was polite as any grandmother could be. Something about her was special. Maybe because her demeanor reminded me of my grandmother, except for the fact that this woman needed a cane to walk.

"Like we told the other lady, we recently found out we were adopted from here sixteen years ago, and we're trying to find out some more information on our past or our real parents," Tony said.

"Unfortunately, Ethel was right. Unless you are eighteen and have filed the proper paperwork, I cannot give you any information. Besides, we would not have your files still. The state claims it after so many years. Have you asked your parents anything?" Ms. Ridgemont asked.

"No, not yet," I said, eyeing Tony, not liking where this is heading already.

"How did you find out you were adopted then? Can't you ask the individual who informed you of this?" she asked us.

"Well, they, our parents, don't know we know yet. I figured if they hadn't told us by now, they probably won't. Besides, we kind of stumbled upon it," Tony said.

"You won't know unless you try. Have this conversation with your parents, and see where it goes. I always say you must try first. Now, sweeties, I am so sorry, but I simply cannot help you," she said, quickly dismissing us, but as she stood up to escort us out, Tony started coughing uncontrollably.

"Oh, Tony, are you okay?" I asked, trying not to laugh at him over acting the part. He clutched his chest and covered his mouth. His cough looked more like a heart attack.

In between his coughing spasms, he asked for some water. She hurriedly got up to go to the kitchen to get him something to drink. As soon as she left, he said, "I will distract her as long as I can. Try and search through those cabinets."

"Yeah, I got the cue," I said.

While he kept her busy, I fumbled through the metal file cabinet against the back wall as quickly as I could. There were only financial paperwork on legalities and stuff I didn't understand. Since that was a no-go, I checked out the table along the front wall and the windowsill behind her chair, but there was nothing other than some funky decorations. Lastly, her messy desk stacked with finances and legalities like in the cabinet also was a bust.

In fact, the only thing I gathered in her office was dust—on the cabinet, her desk, even the chairs, which we had to wipe off before sitting down. Was this not her main office but a storage room, and where did they keep the files on the children? In fact, where are the children? I jumped back into my seat as soon as I heard some commotion down the hallway.

"Sorry about that. Thanks for the water. Allergies, you know," Tony explained to Ms. Ridgemont.

"That is okay, but you should really get that taken care of. Is there anything else I can do for you two?" she asked us but still walked toward the front door.

"Can we get a tour of the facility to see if it brings back any memories?" I asked, almost begging.

"I am sorry, dear, I doubt you would remember being so young, but this is not a good time anyhow. The kids will be back from their day trip soon. I have much to do maybe next time," Ms. Ridgemont said, opening the door for us to leave.

We said our good-byes after she practically kicked us out, and we walked away disappointed. Tony stopped me after we walked a block. "Did you find anything useful?" "No, not really. What struck me as odd was her office was extremely dusty," I said.

"So she's an old dusty lady. I'm sure it's on her to-do list. I mean any paperwork or anything unusual or on us?" Tony asked.

I don't know why the dust bothered me so much, but it did. Something was off with this place. I could feel it. I shook my head no.

"Let's do this. We sneak in through the back and investigate the basement for old files. Before I headed to the kitchen, I checked below the stairs, and there was a door which I'm sure leads to a basement," Tony said.

Now after being inside, I thought the next thing to do was break in since we quickly hit a roadblock, but I felt the others needed to be involved too. "Okay, I'm in, but we should call the others and bring them in on this."

"Come on, we can do it ourselves. I say we make a move before the kids get back so there are less people," he said.

"I get it, but if something is going on, they should be involved. It's only right, especially since we all went the night I wanted to go," I said.

"Here's the deal. If we get in and find something, then we call in reinforcements. Come on,

175

Connor, we're so close. Let's do this," he pleaded with me.

"Fine, I'm in," I said, hoping I wouldn't live to regret it, but something told me we needed to do this if we ever wanted some answers.

Chapter 18

We set off cutting through the woods, which led to the back of the house. We disappeared in the woods. I know it sounds crazy, but we very well couldn't take the chance of someone seeing us vanish on the street.

We then set off toward the back of the house, and just as Tony suspected, the back door was unlocked. He claims that in a small town like this, no one ever locks their doors. I didn't ask how he even knew that.

We opened the back door slowly and snuck in. Inside, to the left of the back entrance, was a door under the stairwell. Tony pointed to it and mouthed, "Basement." He was dead-on.

I actually found this to be exciting, exhilarating. I half expected the basement door to make a high-pitched creaking noise like in the movies when we opened it, but it didn't.

Tiptoeing down the wooded stairs was a challenge. Every so often, it would make a noise under the pressure of our weight, and stopping each time the steps made a noise took us a long-drawn-out minute getting down to the basement.

It was creepy, dusty, and dim down here; but there was some light shining through two small windows. There were two industrial-sized washers and dryers to the left. Let's not forget the seriously creepy boiler. Eeek! Boilers and their big mouths.

Then there were old odds and ends on shelves near the dryer, folded clothes, books scattered in the far corner and on a huge antique bookcase, a wooden dresser, baskets filled with shoes or clothes, and old artwork but not much else. All bound by the cold slab of concrete walls.

We both jumped back, startled when a cat hissed in our direction. I guess animals really can see things that go bump in the night, or in our case, the daytime.

We started searching for whatever, hoping to find something of interest. I was looking through the bookcase, on shelves, and in drawers. I was hoping there were papers that could lead us in any direction.

I had not a clue what Tony was doing. He was feeling up the walls. He watches way too many spy movies.

"Hey, look, I found something," he said.

Maybe spy movies come in handy after all. "What did you find?" I ran over to where he was.

"There is a draft in the wall here and on the floor. Feel it. That means there is a room behind this door." He showed me what he felt, and sure enough, there was a draft. "I figured the basement was too small compared to the size of the house. Help me find a latch," Tony asked.

Good catch. We searched the walls, the nearby panels, and ceiling, but nothing. At first we were stumped, but then it dawned on me—the bookcase. I've seen a spy movie or two myself.

On the bookcase, I remembered there was a small statue that didn't have any dust on it. I ran over and pulled on it. It gave, and as luck would have it, so did the back wall where Tony felt the draft.

He moved out of the way, as the door opened, and we looked at each other as if we hit the jackpot.

Unfortunately, it made such a rumbling commotion that the door at the top of the stairs popped open. That little old woman, Ms. Ridgemont, ran down the stairs so fast, I thought she was going to fall.

"Who's there?" she asked.

I was so glad we decided to stay invisible. Rushing down the stairs, I swear she looked right at me but turned away at the last minute and headed toward the secret door that was open.

After searching through the hidden room, she went to the bookcase where I was standing, but this time she didn't appear to see me and pulled on the statue to shut the door. The cat leaped right on her shoulders from the bookcase, startling her.

"Oh, Ms. Kitty, you nearly gave this old lady a heart attack. Did you open the door? Let's go back upstairs. I do not even know how you got down here." She coddled the cat and carried Ms. Kitty back upstairs with her.

After they were gone, I took my first breath in what felt like five minutes. I fell against the wall, thankful we weren't caught.

"That was close. Some old lady, huh, does she still run track or something?" I was being sarcastic, but it was odd that an old woman like her moved that fast.

I suggested we do like her and get out of here quick. We crept back upstairs and out the back door. In the woods, we came visible and walked toward the park.

In the car, around lots of people, we decided to call the others and explain what happened and see if they would meet us.

He first called Byron, figuring he would be game, and if he came, so would Willow, then Cheyenne would follow suit. It happened just as he figured, but Byron said that he would explain it to Willow on their way there since they were going out anyway. That came only after a million questions as to why we didn't wait and more details as to what happened.

Next was Cheyenne, who was beyond mad at him for going and especially since he came with me. He finally laid into her. He told her about the way she has been acting toward the both of us and that he had enough. To sum it up, if she kept it up, the four of us would figure things out on our own and leave her out.

About time he set her straight. I sat there shocked. She didn't beg, she didn't whine; she simply said fine and hung up.

Then we waited.

Chapter 19

Figuring it would take them at least two hours to get here, Tony suggested going back to the fair and make an evening of it. On the way there, he held my hand without saying a word, which I was okay with. I patted my stomach a few times when the natives became restless.

It was a nice little walk, with the breeze cooling things down a bit even though the record high today was ninety-eight degrees in the shade. My palms were sweaty, but Tony didn't seem to notice or mind.

We passed guys setting up a stage for a band and sectioning off an area for the fireworks tonight. More people were here now than before since the sun no longer instantaneously burst you into flames; it only slowly melted you.

The fair was packed with screaming kids, long lines, and clowns making balloons. Tony asked me if I wanted my face painted after busting me staring at the kids. I did but told him I wasn't a child.

"Oh, come on, you know you want to," Tony said, teasing me and tickling me to death.

"I will if you will," I said trying to tickle him back, but he wasn't ticklish. Unfair.

We walked around, deciding on what we wanted to do first: eat, which I brought up, or rides, which he brought up.

"Better yet, how about a big stuffed animal?" he asked me.

"No argument there, but are you sure you're man enough for the challenge?"

"Man, huh. Pick it, and I promise you I will win it," he said with that oh-so-devilish grin of his.

"Fine."

I spotted the biggest stuffed animal I could find, a big blue bear, and it was so cute. The game was to hit the moving object with this pea-sized ball that if it did hit the object, it probably wouldn't fall anyway.

It was the hardest game at the fair, and only one person was on the wall of winners while everyone else was on the wall of shame. Plus there were ten levels to get to the bear I wanted.

"Bet it's yours, but what do I get in return?" he asked. "Huh, I don't know. What do you want?"

I asked, almost regretting it, praying he couldn't hear my heart beating

out of my chest.

"For every level passed, I get a kiss for that long. So level 1 gets me a minute kiss, level 2 gets me a two-minute kiss, then so on and so on."

I'm only fifteen, but he's going to give me a heart attack. "Sure," I managed to exhale.

Tony stepped up to the game and placed his bet with the man behind the counter. "My girl wants that bear right there on the top and nothing else."

His girl, he said. His girl. I should be mad because he called me a girl plus we never discussed exclusivity, but I didn't mind. When he glanced back at me, I giggled like a little schoolgirl. Did I just do that? Oh, wow. Now I get what Ebony is talking about.

The man called others over to play and watch, and as soon as enough people participated, the man rang a loud bell. One man said he wanted the big prize for his girl too. "It's a challenge. Let the games begin." The man said over the microphone.

Tony hit them right on, never missing a beat as the other four participants struggled, but only Tony and two others went on to level 2. I cheered so loud, you would have thought he won the big prize already. The man tried to hand Tony a little prize, but he shook his head no.

The same three went on to level 2, 3, 4, but only Tony and his main competitor hung in there. More people showed up and crowded around, cheering him on. At this point the man was playing head games, telling them not to give up and talking about the pressure of disappointing their women. Level 7 came and went without his rival, who missed his last shot.

It was Tony who hung in there on level 8, then 9, and finally the tenth round. People were quiet, I held my breath and Tony stayed focused. I knew he had skills and a little special help, but honestly I didn't think he would get this far.

Tony went all the way being the second winner ever. I was awestruck, grinning from ear to ear, holding my bear. People cheered him, patted him on the back, and this one man even came over offered him an opportunity to try out for his baseball team.

We walked off from the crowd to a seated area. "You like it?" he asked.

"Yes, but honestly I didn't think you were going all the way. I mean…" I said, but he shut me up with a kiss. It wasn't as long as I expected, but it was nice.

"I will collect my prize later. Let me have Sci-Fi Jr. here and take him to the car, okay?" he asked.

"That's not his name, and yeah, it's sort of big," I said, knowing full well that's the name I will give it.

"Besides, that roller coaster is calling my name," he trotted off, pointing to the tallest ride here like that was going to happen.

Waiting for him to come back, I got that familiar feeling that someone was watching me. I stood up to check my surroundings, but no one was around. It was as strong as the night I first met the others. The sense of feeling someone near had become compelling more so than before. When Tony got back, I didn't say anything. I'd rather let us enjoy the day.

We discussed which rides to take, and even though I protested, somehow Tony talked me into getting on a roller coaster. Bad move.

It took its time slowly going uphill, but as soon as we reached the top, it dropped fast and hard, taking us under the tracks. My stomach was in my throat. I squeezed the life out of Tony, who, by the way, loved the ride. He was howling like the other nuts on this trip in purgatory. It went on forever, never ending. I think I passed out once or twice. Finally, after it was over, Tony had to practically hold me up—my legs were jelly.

"That was great, huh?" Tony asked. "Are you nuts?"

"Aw, come on, it wasn't that bad. The next one will be calmer. I promise."

He lied. The next few rides were some pirate's swing, a free drop, followed by a spinning UFO. I told him that was it. I was a good sport, but now it's my turn.

I made him get on the carousel with me, which he didn't like and told me as much. His horse had a pink saddle, and I told him he looked pretty. I forced him to take the haunted ride of nonscary creatures, then the teacups a girly kids ride.

He was so mad about the teacups, he kept trying to get off during the ride. We laughed so hard the whole time, with me trying to take pictures of us. The kids on the ride didn't find us so funny, but to us it was a blast.

"Thanks for being a sport about it," I said. "Yeah don't forget payback is a..."

"Hey, I was a good sport too. It's getting late, so what now, food?" I so hoped he agreed.

"One last ride, then we can go eat, but you have to cover your eyes, please."

"Since you asked me so nicely, I will play along." I covered my eyes, complaining the whole time and threatening his life.

"Now open them. It's time to collect my prize," he said. My mouth fell. The sign to the ride read "the Tunnel of Love." I could not stop blushing as he led me to our seat. Before the ride started, he pulled off a silver chain from around his neck and put it on me. It held his extremist champion ring, which by comparison is almost valued as

a fat diamond ring. I didn't know what to say. "Will you be my girl?" he asked.

"Yes."

We never once checked out the scenery; we kissed the whole time. The attendant had to clear his throat to get our attention. The ride had finished, but we didn't even notice.

It was raining out now, so we took shelter for a few until we agreed it was time to eat. He took me to very nice Italian restaurant. Apparently, when he dropped off Junior, he made dinner reservations for two.

We sat in a corner, away from the others, closely snuggling. I don't think our hands, arms, or legs stopped touching all night. I ordered shrimp parmesan and he, baked ziti, sharing everything between us. The day turned out to be better than I could have imagined.

"Thank you, Tony. I had a great time with you today." "I did too. I love spending time with you, Connor. I hope you now get that?" Tony asked, but before I could answer, his cell buzzed. It was Byron, asking where we were. I nodded yes to him as he spoke, and he smiled back. He told them we would be there in five. He paid the check, and we left.

Chapter 20

By now, the rain had stopped, and we met up with them in the parking lot by Tony's car.

This time, everyone had on T-shirts, jeans, and sneakers. I was so grateful and surprised they didn't dress up since the goal tonight was to sneak around. Actually, I was really surprised Willow would agree to do this at all. I pulled her aside and asked just that. "What made you agree to this? I figured you would run in the opposite direction, no offense."

"None taken, and trust me, I tried but didn't really have a choice since Byron told me when we were en route. I should have known something was up when he called me right before he picked me up and told me to dress down. I figured we were going indoor rock climbing or something. I'm not too happy about it, but I don't want to be on the outs," she said.

"Well, I'm glad you came even if you're not," I said. "Oh, by the way, don't worry about Cheyenne. She will get over her issues. I had to hear an earful on the way over here. Like Tony said, she is rough around the edges, but she is actually cool once you get to know her," Willow said.

Somehow, I didn't believe that, or maybe she's cool only when that someone is not in her way. "What is her story anyway? Most people don't walk around attacking people they don't even know," I asked.

She leaned against Byron's car and took a deep breath. That deep breath clued me in that I was going to hear an earful too. "She is a product of her upbringing. She is the only child. Her family is never, and I mean never, around. Her mom stays six months out of the year in Japan visiting family, and when she is here, she is too busy for Cheyenne. Her father is constantly working, but he avoids his wife. She is far from warm. I don't think I have ever seen her smile. On the other hand, even though her father is nice, he always looks distracted. So basically, her nanny, who is as rigid as they come, raised her. The poor girl wants or needs for nothing financially. Parental affection is not their agenda. She would have to come to my house for get-togethers or holidays.

My family is so opposite of hers, thank goodness."

"Wow, what a mouthful. Wait, so you and Cheyenne knew each other before all this business happened?" I was stunned; their personalities were so opposite. I couldn't imagine Cheyenne sitting around a roaring fire singing cheery holiday songs. I envision her ice picking cheery holiday people instead.

"Yes, can you believe it?" she said, tapping my arm ever so gently as if we were two ladies at a tea party discussing this week's book. "We are so different, but for some reason, we clicked, and maybe this is why." She was referring to us five somehow feeling connected.

"What I am trying to say is she is not the type to beat around the bush, and she doesn't believe in holding her tongue, not for anyone. That is something I have been trying to work on her for years. The thing about her is once she likes you, she doesn't let go. It's not you, Connor. She is afraid of losing Tony as a friend. For her, friends are hard to come by. Girls hate her because she refuses to play the silly little social games. Oh, don't get me wrong, she has friends, but they are more superficial and not like Tony and me," Willow explained.

Wow. In a way, I sort of felt sorry for her. "Her family life sucks. Mine is so boringly normal compared to hers— who am I kidding—compared to anybody," I said.

"Anyway, ever since this adoption thing she's so gung ho on doing this. Maybe her real parents will be different. Maybe they would want to meet her. She hasn't come out and said it, but I know her well enough to know that is what she is hoping for," Willow said.

I was about to say something when Cheyenne walked over. "What's the secrecy all about?" She was directing the question to Willow.

"We were discussing what happened tonight in the house." Willow sounded a little more enthusiastic than she should, possibly feeling guilty discussing Cheyenne's business with me.

"Oh, well, obviously nothing great, or we wouldn't be here to help," Cheyenne said, still only talking to Willow as if I didn't exist.

Woooow. There went that little bit of pity I felt for her fly right out the window. "Well, obviously something worthwhile, or we wouldn't have had all of you to come out here. Besides, I don't recall anyone begging you to come." What a witch. I walked off and overheard Willow telling her to behave.

I went by Tony and Byron, who were going over tonight's events again and suggested we get started on a plan. We gathered in a discreet spot off the parking lot, opposite side of the fair, to discuss how we were going to get in without anyone hearing us. The only way was to get the two older women, the kids, and if anyone else was inside, out of the house.

Someone suggested calling the fire department, which would work, but that would get them out the house and not give us enough time to look around and get back out. Besides, we would have to be able to shut the door from inside the room, if that was even an option, before the firefighters came to look around the basement.

Then I said, "How do we know they are not at the fair tonight? If I had a group of kids, that is exactly what I would do. There is supposed to be entertainment and fireworks tonight. What kid wouldn't love to see that?"

"That may be true, but we still need a backup plan. I say if they are there, we call the fire department, who will force them to leave the premises. That way we can sneak downstairs," Tony said.

"And with the fireworks tonight, we can only hope the firemen think the slight rumble they feel from the door opening is the fireworks show. If the room is as big as we think, Tony, we are going to need more time than what the firefighters need to search the house. Another issue is someone has to stay out in order to close the door from the outside. Plus be the lookout," Byron said.

"Not me," Willow said, biting her bottom lip.

I knew the only logical choice was me. I told them about my hearing incident this morning and agreed to be the lookout.

"What! We've been together all day, and I'm just now hearing about this?" Tony picked me up by my waist and swinging me around three times before setting me back down. "That is great, really, really great."

"It slipped my mind really, I don't know how but it did." I knew exactly how, the kiss. "The thing is it only happened once, and I haven't had time to practice, but when I concentrated on it this afternoon, I was able to do it. No problem."

"So what's that make, three abilities now?" Byron said, smiling at me and giving me a big hug. "I don't know what that is all about, but I am glad you are certainly on our team." That was pretty much the census from everyone, and being that Cheyenne didn't say anything negative, I took it positively.

"Try it now and see if you can hear a conversation at the fair," Byron suggested.

The fair was about a quarter of a mile away, which was further than I tried today, but I did it with no problem. As a matter of fact, I could hear several conversations and distinguish them all. For some reason, this was much easier to control than telekinesis. I guess some abilities come easier than others do.

The plan was set. Plan A: I would be the lookout while they searched inside the room. First, we would check if anyone was home. If not, go in and start searching immediately, and if lucky, we would get out before anyone came home.

Plan B: If no one were home initially, they would go straight to the room, and I would shut them in. If anyone came home while still inside the secret room, I would wait it out, depending on how much time we planned. We agreed to wait and see how big the room was before setting a time limit so they could search as much as possible.

When that time was up, I would call the fire department from the park and not my cell, since Tony knew 911 tracks every call, then race back to the house. Once the cavalry cleared the staff members and kids out of the house, I would let them out of the room.

We figured the fireworks would be over long before I needed to get them out, so there wouldn't be any noise coverage when the door opened. The rumble will at least be noticeable on the first floor, so I hope we can get the door shut before the police or firefighters race downstairs to investigate the disturbance.

Plan C: However, if they were home initially, we would call the fire department twice: once to get in, and another to get out. While I used a pay phone in the park, the others would wait at the house for the police and the firefighters to show up. Once the house cleared, they would creep downstairs and open the door. Figuring cell reception sucked in the basement, Byron would message me at the top of the stairs an estimated length of time they agreed upon, pull the statue to close them in and hurry into the room as I raced back to be the lookout. They were not the greatest plans, but it's the best we could do in a short amount of time. It was all about the timing.

Before reaching the house, Tony told me he wasn't happy I was the one staying behind to do all the footwork and be the lookout. I told him we had no other choice and was cool with it. Not true, but I was the best person to do the job, so I had to step up to the plate and handle it.

In the woods behind the house, we checked if the coast was clear. I didn't hear a sound inside the house, and neither did Cheyenne see anyone.

When the back door opened for Tony, he looked back at me with a raised brow. He obviously was surprised like me; after what happened today, I swore they would have locked it, if not for the fact alone that no one was home. Once again, my spidey senses were tingling.

We raced to the basement door and down the stairs. Not taking any time, I yanked on the statue opening the door to the secret room, letting the others in. A light was on already, so we didn't have to waste time looking for one.

The room was huge, about half the size of the basement. The walls were made of concrete, but it looked like any office with a desk covered in notes, a stack of folders, and a typewriter, but this one was an old-fashioned cast-iron one.

There were three lamps, two leather chairs, five tall filing cabinets lined against the right wall, and a tall bookshelf like the one out here, but there wasn't a statue on it. I'm sure there is a latch to close the door from the inside; we just didn't have time to search for it.

Since the room was huge, we agreed on three hours of search and any seizure if necessary. Of course, the cell phones were useless down here like we thought. We synchronized our watches, and Byron set the timer on his phone, then I locked them in.

As the door rumbled shut, it felt like I was shutting them inside a large tomb. Standing on the outside, I felt the impact of them being gone. What to do for the next three hours?

Not caring for basements, a.k.a. boilers, I went upstairs to look around, hoping to find something of significance to our cause. There were a few lights on, so I didn't have to walk around in the dark.

I came to an office next to the one we were in earlier today, which could have been the rude woman's, Ethel's, but there weren't any pictures, so who knows. Come to think of it, there weren't any pictures in Ms. Ridgemont's office either.

I thought all older women had pictures; interesting, and not in a good way. I was in there for about fifteen minutes, but it was clear there was nothing of importance to our cause, so I moved on.

I felt like a little snack, so I headed to the kitchen to see if I could sneak something. I passed Ms. Ridgemont's office on my right and the stairs to my left, then turned down the hallway we noticed earlier. There was only a small bathroom and a wall filled with old paintings, not much else.

In the kitchen, there were some chocolate-chip cookies in a jar on the counter, so I helped myself. I hopped onto the counter, wasting time eating some yummy homemade cookies.

The kitchen wallpaper was baby blue and white stripes. There was a window across from me with yellow curtains, and in front of it was a small table for two. To my right, a silver fridge sat next to a side door leading to the outside. On the opposite wall of the fridge was a small metal shelf and a clean silver stove, under me white countertops surrounding a white porcelain sink, with matching white cabinets along the wall above me.

This kitchen needs a serious makeover. I finished my snack and ventured through a door leading to a dining area.

This room is where all wood came to die. The dining table sat eight wooden chairs around a wooden table. There was wood from the walls, picture frames, to the furniture. Even a wooden china cabinet filled with crystal glassware and blue-and-white porcelain plates.

I walked across the hall to the sitting room. It was a nice-sized room that contained two flowery couches, two green-and-yellow striped sitting chairs, some lamps, and more awful-looking furniture in the back. The two bay windows were cool though.

I plopped down on one of the couches and checked my phone. So far, I wasted about forty minutes of my time and was beyond bored to death. Losing my mind waiting for the earth to rotate, I decided to go upstairs to see what other exciting adventures awaited me.

I must be feeling brave because something about an unfamiliar house, especially one that's empty, creeped me out, but this place was exceptionally eerie. Possibly because of the settling noises, the old-fashioned furniture, the stale smell, and the dull lights that were casting shadows I could swear were following me.

A small light lit the stairwell leading up into who knows what. At the top of the stairs was an open area, so I stopped for a minute to get my bearings. There was a bathroom directly in front of me, and the upstairs split into two hallways: one went left and the other went right; I decided to go right.

A light streamed from one of the rooms, giving me a little light in the dark hallway. On my left was a built-in wall shelf, which held about six white towels, six washcloths, six hand towels, nothing else. Three sixes, not cool. Walking past it, I stopped in front of the first room to my right.

The pink lampshade on the nightstand was casting a pink glow, dimly lighting the room. Walking into what appeared to be the girl's room because it was pink, and I mean pink, from the walls to the carpet, to the canopies over two twin-sized beds. The bedspreads were pink with white flowers, matching the throw rugs on the side of each bed. On the far side of the room was a, you guessed it, pink door to a closet filled with girl clothes.

The furniture was a matching white set, from the bed, the nightstand, to the dressers and even two little rocking chairs. The rocking chairs sat to the left of the closet holding porcelain dolls in each one. One doll had a crack along her face from her left eye to her lip. Holy creep factor, Batman!

Keeping my distance from the dolls, I bent down to look at a bookshelf far enough away from the chairs. The books were old but well kept. A cute closed wooden toy chest sat next to the bookshelf. I wasn't about to open it in case there were more dolls inside.

Behind me, the lamp on the nightstand started blinking uncontrollably, as if it were having a spasm. I pivoted to look at it but then felt eyes on the back of my head, I quickly turned back around, and there in the corner stood a life-size clown smiling back at me. I leaped up and ran out. Both a clown and porcelain dolls, that's just wrong.

In the hall, I passed another girl's room, I assumed, since the colors were yellow and white. What is with these color schemes? Females do like darker colors, you know; my favorite color is midnight blue, like the color of the classic Mustang.

I decided not to venture in, being that it is probably the exact replica of the pink room but instead headed to a door at the end of the hall. I turned the knob and pulled on it, but it would not open.

I kept at it until a cold chill ran down my spine. I stopped and turned around but saw nothing. I stood there a minute, waiting but brushed it off, telling myself it was my nerves. Get it together, Connor.

I decided to walk back down the hall, the way I came in, and go into what appeared to be the boy's room, since the colors were blue and red.

A Do Not Disturb sign hung from the door handle. Cute. I walked in to waste more time and see how they decorated this room. The walls covered with wallpaper were of different sports memorabilia. It seemed like a typical boy's room with trophies, sports equipment, and toy model airplanes hanging from the ceiling.

Wait a minute. I looked back at the trophies, checking the nameplates; they didn't have names on any of them.

I heard a scraping noise by the hallway, so I quickly turned around but, once again, saw nothing. Either I'm losing my mind or just paranoid. At least that's what I thought until I noticed the Do Not Disturb sign swinging back and forth from the doorknob.

Someone is in this house with us, worse yet, in this room with me now. I heard nothing nor did I see anyone, but I sensed it, and it was not a welcoming feeling.

I had my hands up, braced for anything that came at me. I slowly eased my way back across the room, my back close to the wall, inching toward the door, breath on hold. As soon as both feet touched the hallway, the door slammed shut behind me, and all the lights in the house died.

In total darkness, I jetted full speed in the hall and down the stairs, and then swung open the basement door, popping the hinges, the whole time sensing someone near me.

What were we thinking breaking into this house? We clearly did not think this through.

I pulled on the statue opening the door to the room. Tony was the first one out, with Byron a close second, both asking what gives.

Out of breath, I told them to wrap it up now, but they stood there looking bewildered.

"Now! We have company, and we are not welcomed." I then pulled on the statue to shut the door, not waiting around. They quickly wrapped it up and hurried out as the door was closing in on them. They followed suit, running after me, no questions asked, the whole time still sensing something near me.

Chapter 21

I ran to the woods nonstop, not caring who was behind me. My mind was reeling from all the possibilities of what could've happened to us tonight. Who was that, or what was that? Knowing something was there the whole time but not able to see it shook me from the inside out. It could have killed us, me, especially by myself. It was so angry.

I heard them calling my name, but I wanted to keep on going until I no longer felt this way. Someone grabbed hold of me, wrestling me to the ground, but I resisted making contact with someone, fighting to get him or her off me. I was in fight-or-flight mode and didn't even know or care who it was. I was just about up until someone else jumped on me, holding me down.

It was Byron and Tony sitting on top of me, shaking me out of it. They refused to get up until I promised to calm down. I told them they had three seconds to get off me or I would sneak into their rooms at night and stab them each while they slept. They did.

I got up, wiping the dirt off. We were deeper into the woods, opposite the direction of the park, but the moon gave us enough light to see. I no longer sensed anything unfamiliar near us, so I relaxed a bit but still very much cautious.

"Sorry, Connor, but you kept running in the wrong direction, and we thought you would never stop," Tony said, bent over panting. "Dang, girl, you can run. What happened back there?"

I apologized to Byron for punching him, and he accepted, a little out of breath too. "It's okay, but I wanted to make sure the others were together before I caught you. Nice right hook. You're feisty for someone so little. Please do explain," Byron said.

"There was someone, something in that house with us!" I all but yelled it, pointing in the direction of the house we could no longer see. I started pacing back and forth, taking deep breaths, shaking my head. I explained the rest of what happened, and they listened without any interruptions. "I kept having bad feelings about this, but I kept brushing it off, saying it was my paranoia. Wrong."

"Wait, what, someone was in that house with us?" Willow said, looking around as if she felt someone now watching her.

"I no longer sense anyone near us, but that really doesn't mean anything, being I didn't sense it earlier tonight when we first broke in. None of us did," I said.

"You did say that Ms. Ridgemont moved too fast for an old lady. She most likely has abilities too, may it be good or bad. Maybe it was her," Tony said, reminding me.

"I vaguely remember you saying that, only the parts that reeked of possibilities," Byron said. "Willow, you made a good point in the basement the other night about us all adopted around the same time. How rare is that? When you think about it, chances are they themselves have abilities too. It only makes logical sense to me that they would since they had to take care of us."

"Yeah, he is right. Let's face it, we were so excited about finding something out, we never stopped to think what we could find," Cheyenne said stressing the word "could". "Maybe they are related to us or at least know our families." "Well, if we are related to them, then they won't harm us, right?" Willow asked, rubbing her arms.

"No, guys, listen. That in there," I said, pointing again, "was not the women we met today. It was someone, something else. I don't know how I know, I just do. Who or whatever that was, was very angry."

"I got a chance to look around when you were in the hidden room, and I think this house is a front for who knows what. I don't believe any kids live here. Plus, look, the woods practically surrounds this place. For what reason? The nearest neighbor is about a quarter of a mile away. Why, for seclusion's sake?" I went into detail about the inconsistencies I saw in the house, like old furniture, nameless trophies, well-kept books, and to think of it, the absurdly clean stove that looked like it was never used. There wasn't an ounce of child's clutter anywhere. I reminded Tony of the dust in the offices and told him there was a reason why it bothered me.

"None of this makes any sense really. Who could they be?" Willow said.

"No, this doesn't make sense, Willow, and that is why we are here to figure all this craziness out. We didn't plan this well, but we all saw an opportunity and took it," Byron said, this time not so much consoling Willow but explaining the importance.

"Well, did you guys find anything important in the room?" I asked.

"We found our folders grouped together with others named Bynder, Tochia, Tanzia, Shak, Selene, and Khan. There was one on your friend's adopted brother, Vincent, attached to a folder that had a big X across the front. The name on the folder said Herina or Frina—not sure. Plus a lot of other names none of us heard of before, but who knows what we could have found if we had more time? Oh yeah, that same gibberish we saw in the basement," Tony said.

"The thing that concerns me was the lack of consistency. There was paperwork with dates going back thousands of years ago, but the majority of the dates spanned every two hundred years or so from then to now, with few dates in between. How old is this place, and what happened during those lulls?" Byron asked.

"That gibberish in our folders ties us to this place and possibly those women you two met earlier. I believe this place is very old from the black-and-white photos I found in old-fashioned hatboxes, old paintings of people riding horse and buggies. Also, I found this book of disfigured people and distorted-looking animals with that same writing next to their pictures. We're connected to something deeper than we could ever have imagined. Now I wish we hadn't sat on this so long," Cheyenne said.

"Why doesn't anyone come to us?" I asked. "What really pisses me off is we have to figure all of this out ourselves." "I don't care anymore. Can we just go?" Willow asked. No one answered her, so she tried to ask again, but I cut her off. "I'm sorry, Willow, but no, absolutely not. We only know of one other, so I say we go pay him a visit. Let's track him down and see if that was him inside the house with us tonight. If not, then we force some answers

out of him to find out what he knows.

"Who's 'he,' that insane boy from your school who attacked you? No way. I would like to avoid him, thank you very much," Willow said, looking between Byron and me. "I'm not feeling so well. I want to go home, Byron," she said, pleading with him.

Byron said, "Any other night, yes, but not tonight. I say we see if he has some answers, or better yet, maybe he is able to control his abilities in a way where no one can see him unless he wants to."

"I agree too, Willow. They have a point. We need to find this boy and make him talk," Cheyenne said.

"Ditto, the only thing is we don't know where he lives," Tony said. "Unless we make it two for two and break into the school to get it."

"That won't be necessary, I have it. The other day in the principal's office, Scott, that is his name. I meant to tell you in the basement last night, but Vincent's folder caught me off guard. I saw him with Mr. Stuckey when Mrs. Potts, our office administrator, opened the door. His file was on her desk, but she is so dense, she forgot to take it to him when she got up to tell him why I was there, so I peeked in. His address is in here," I motioned toward my head.

"As in one of the names on a folder we found last night. I say we don't go if we are all not in agreement, and I'm not. I'm not going," Willow demanded. "We are talking mad. We don't know this boy. Who is to say he will be alone? I say we discuss this tomorrow, then decide what to do."

"Why are you fighting this so hard? You're not the only one involved in this. Think about it, if no one knew about you, Byron, and I before, they do now. If they won't come to us, I say we seek them out. We have sat on this for too long. I want answers, Willow, even if you don't," Cheyenne said, a little irritated with Willow.

"You will be safe with us, Willow, don't worry," Byron said. "I'm hoping if we keep stirring up trouble, maybe they won't have any other choice and come to us."

For the second time tonight, Willow didn't have a choice in the matter, especially since Byron drove her and he wanted in. I felt bad for her, but she needs to learn to face reality. Like I can talk, but at least my not facing reality is not holding me back from searching for more answers.

Chapter 22

Since Scott lived closest to me, we drove the cars to my house and parked. On the way there, I called my parents to make sure they were not home but at the neighbor's party as planned. They go to this party every year, so I knew they would be gone all night. Tony and Cheyenne parked in front of my house, then we hopped into Byron's vehicle, and we all rode together to Scott's.

It was around nine on a Saturday night, so hopefully, he would be home; we doubted it, but we hoped. We were there in five minutes.

We parked down the block and crept into his yard. He lived on a corner with no side neighbor, so we could hop the fence without anyone calling the cops. Willow remained the lookout this time, which she preferred.

Cutting across the backyard, we stayed low and close to the house. The yard had a pool, lounge furniture, and the typical accessories like a grill, a table set, and decorations.

We peeked through each window downstairs, but his dad was the only one we saw in the living room. He had a bottle in one hand and a glass in the other and kept nodding off. I was betting he had a little too much to drink.

Cheyenne didn't see anyone else upstairs, but after what happened earlier, that didn't mean anything. The sliding door to the back was unlocked, and Tony wanted to check the house more thoroughly. I swear he had a death wish. I told him I had a better idea and to follow me. I waved them back to the fence so I could tell them my plan.

"I'm going to knock on the door to see if he is home. If he is, I will ask him to come out. I doubt he can resist another possible fight, and according to his file, he never passes one up. If he's not, then I will tell his dad I was supposed to meet him and ask if he knows where he is, okay?" I hopped the fence before they could object and ran to the front door.

I rang the bell, ignoring them calling out to me from the bushes. His dad answered the door, reeking of alcohol. I asked him if Scott was home, and as suspected, he was not. I asked if he knows

217

where he is because I was supposed to meet up with him. He rambled on about not able to keep up with him and told me to try the old factory warehouses on the water and something about fighting. I said thank you and jogged off.

After giving me a scolding, Byron drove off under Tony's directions to the warehouses. "He's talking about the cage fights that go on there. I've heard of it but have never gone. It is supposed to be brutal. If he cage fights, Connor, then he took it easy on you."

"Gee, thanks, Tony." I held my own. When I was younger, I always got into trouble for beating up boys. Most little girls liked it when little boys wanted to kiss them; not me. Instead, I liked it when they kissed the dirt.

Pulling into the lot, I confirmed hearing fighting inside the warehouse. We parked under a broken post away from the other cars. We decided to infiltrate by invisibility since teens weren't allowed anyway.

Making our way to the building, we walked around until we found an opening and squeezed through a metal door that was left slightly open. There was barely any light inside, so Cheyenne led us through a maze of construction and debris. Finally making our way to the lights, we passed two guards and entered a huge room where the fighting took place.

A wave of must wafted over us, making me want to run in the opposite direction. Cheyenne, Willow, and I had to cover our noses at first. Tony and Byron hardly noticed. Typical.

It was jam-packed with adults yelling, shoving, and yes, even spitting at each other, rooting for either opponent fighting inside a barbed-wired cage in the middle of the room. There must have been about a hundred people in here tonight. Some poor person kept getting knocked down after struggling to get back up.

We managed to dodge waving arms and kicking legs while searching for Scott. I spotted him across the way and pointed him out to the others. That area must be where the contenders sit from the sweat, cuts, and bruises; some had already.

Scott sat there calmly, sweat dripping down his face, with a soaked shirt clinging to his back. He had a few cuts but not much else, unlike the others. Honestly, from his lack of expression, he didn't seem to have a care in the world. He could have easily been sitting in the park watching the birds fly by or watching paint dry.

Tony waved us over to a corner away from the crowd. "I don't think he was at the house tonight. From the looks of it, he's been here a while."

"I agree. I doubt he'd have time to get from there to here and have already fought," Byron said.

"Listen, remember when I said someone was following me? I didn't tell you everything. I approached the person one day, but he didn't say anything when I caught him. I asked him what he wanted, but he walked off, never answering me. It was he, Scott. I'm pretty sure he used to go to our school too, but I never knew what happened to him," Cheyenne said.

"He was kicked out due to his odd behavior and constant fighting according to his folder, then transferred to our school," I said.

We heard Scott's name announced by a man holding a microphone, so we made our way back to the commotion. The mention of his name made the crowd grow louder and become more hostile, if possible. Two guys were getting mobbed with bets; they could barely keep up.

Wanting to see him in action, we walked closer to the cage. If he was scared, he didn't show it. He walked in, standing still unlike his opponent, who kept hopping around, boxing and kicking the air.

The opponent was almost twice Scott's size, so I don't know how they matched the fighters. That and the fact he was a teen, even though he appeared older, and everyone else were adults. Then again, this is not legal fighting. Scott was maybe five ten with lean muscle, while this guy was at least six feet and stacked with muscles.

There was a referee in the middle, brave man, making them keep their distance until the bell rang. Once the referee stepped out the gate, it locked; a bell went off, commencing the fight. I didn't want to admit it, but something inside me secretly rooted for Scott. What's wrong with me?

They walked around and around the cage until the opponent went for Scott, and that's when things got ugly.

Scott dodged his advance and punched him right in the nose, causing blood to spew into the air and onto the floor. The man went down. Scott waited patiently off to the side as he recovered.

Scott's opponent got back up, shaking it off, danced around a bit, then swung at Scott, who grabbed his arm and punched him in the gut, causing the guy to crumble to his knees to catch his breath. Once again, Scott politely stood to the side while his opponent recovered. I don't think Scott broke a sweat yet.

The crowd was getting so insanely rowdy that the bouncers—I had not even noticed before now—were trying to contain them.

His opponent managed to get back up, holding on to the cage for support. This time Scott charged first, causing his opponent to backpedal, then the opponent charged, and Scott backpedaled. It went on like that for a while until Scott kicked his opponent in the face, knocking him cross-eyed. The guy hit the ground, and Scott was on top of him, pounding his face in until all you saw was blood.

The poor man didn't even stand a chance. I swore Scott was enjoying this way too much. A bell rang, and two referees came running in to pull Scott off the guy as he lay there limp. Both refs grabbed Scott and yanked him off the bloody guy, but not before Scott kicked his opponent in the face and spat on him.

The crowd was booing and cheering at the same time. It was a madhouse in here. Two more referees came in to carry the guy who was barely breathing out. His face was unrecognizable. Tony was right—he did go easy on me.

After the referees carried Scott's opponent completely out, they announced him the winner, but instead of him taking it all in, he immediately left the gate, collected his winnings, and headed toward the exit. We ran after him, but after fighting through the crowd, we lost him outside. He was nowhere we could see.

We decided to search for him by car in case he cut through a path somewhere by foot. While cutting across the lot, two black SUVs with tinted windows blocked us, driving around and around in a circle until we stopped moving. We huddled together.

The vehicles stopped, but only one driver, a male, got out. "You may reveal yourselves now," and said each of our names. He was a tall muscular man with a bald head, not from old age, but done purposely. He looked familiar to me, but I couldn't place from where.

"Excuse me, my name is Shak, and I assure you that you will not be harmed unless absolutely necessary." We did as ordered.

"Shak, as in one of the names on the folders, Shak. What do you want?" Tony asked.

"Better question, how could you see us? Who are you?" Cheyenne asked.

Ignoring both questions, Shak told us to get in either vehicle.

"No way, buddy, not on your life," I said. "I'm not hopping into a car with a stranger."

Tony grabbed my arm and said, "We know you. You're Ole Man Johnston, the caretaker at our school." A chill ran down my spine. He was right. "But how, why? What is going on?"

When Tony stepped closer to Shak to reiterate, the second driver, another male, got out of the second vehicle, got off the phone, and said, "Get in, or we will forcibly put you in. I have no problem doing the latter of the two. Actually, I would prefer it." He was a tall, muscular man who looked every bit intimidating as intimidating could get, and the scar on his left cheek didn't help.

The second driver walked over to Shak and I overheard him say Scott got away cutting through the woods on foot, so they will check out his usual spots. He then walked back over to the vehicle, appearing more pissed than before.

"I would do as he says. Please get in. That will be the last time I ask," Shak said, smiling as he started to apply black gloves.

I don't remember him asking, but that is irrelevant right now; my safety is, and the fact that he was applying gloves was not a good sign.

The second man opened the back door to his SUV then proceeded to walk toward us. Not wanting to take on two men who obviously meant business, we obliged, and the second man stopped walking.

Somehow, I wound up in the vehicle of the scarier guy with Tony. I'm pretty sure it was Willow who shoved me out the way so she could ride with the nicer of the two mystery men. Probably to get me back for suggesting we follow Scott in the first place. Maybe Byron was right about them coming to us; at least I hope they were on our side, or we're screwed.

We rode in silence to the unknown. I figured asking our chauffeur, but that would be a most likely a waste of time.

I wasn't sure we were heading back toward my house until he turned down my block, but he stopped in front of my neighbor's house, Mrs. Nosy Palmer a.k.a. Secret Service, instead of mine. You have to be kidding me. This keeps getting better and better.

He got out, opening the back door for us. He nodded toward her house, "Walk to the back. I will be right behind you." We got out, no questions asked. The other SUV was nowhere in sight. We walked to the back of the house with the scary man on our heels. Climbing the back stairs, Mrs. Palmer, or whoever she really is, opened the door for us. "Sorry about this, Connor, but we had no other choice. Down the stairs, the two of you." Pointing to her basement door, she sounded like her typical irritating self.

I didn't appreciate the way they were treating us, but we wanted this right, well, answers? Half of me wanted to scream at her and resist, but the other half wanted the truth, so for now I behaved.

I hadn't been in her basement in years, and it looked much different from what I remembered. It was spacious, well lit, and spotless. Now it's decorated in vintage colors like red and white with an orange splash, with perfectly arranged furniture and a few pictures of fruit. Hello, seventies.

"The others will be here soon," was all she said then locked us in.

We looked at one another for a second, like did that door just click. We turned running up the stairs, tripping over each other, trying to get to it first. I banged on it as Tony tried to open it. I started yelling for Mrs. Palmer to come open the door.

"Umm, Connor, I'm pretty sure she is not coming back since she locked us in here in the first place," he said like it was my fault.

"Umm, you don't have to be so sarcastic, you know. It doesn't hurt to try."

"Step back," he ordered. I got out of the way as he went full ram into the door. It didn't even budge. He did it about five more times until he gave up, holding his shoulder, expressing a full array of colorful words.

"I thought they brought us here to give us answers. His name was Shak, as in one of the names on the folders grouped with ours." He continued beating the door with his fist. "That's definitely not wood, more like reinforced titanium."

"Okay, calm down. I don't know, Tony, they kind of didn't tell me that part of the plan. Yeah, I thought we were going to get answers too. She said the others should be here soon, so let's wait and see what happens."

We said we would give it fifteen minutes. For now, we searched for something to break down the door, but we found nothing. There were only two couches, two chairs, and an empty bar, as in not even any bottles. The pictures were more like paintings, which meant no glass for weapons. Aggravated and disgusted, we sat on the steps trying to figure out what to do next.

"No, I hate to say it, but I never suspected her of anything except being nosy," I said when Tony asked about suspecting Mrs. Palmer of anything.

"What about the so-called janitor, Ole Man Johnston. Who would have suspected him of anything with his fake limp? I would see him around my neighborhood, thinking he lived by me. Man, I'm pissed. For months we've been digging for answers, and there they were right in front us this whole time," Tony said.

"Shh, I hear something." Running back upstairs, I listened. There was a car pulling into the driveway and the garage door closing. I hope that it was the others. It had only been five minutes, but it felt more like hours.

I gave the play-by-play to Tony, who suggested we should run out as soon as the door opened. I agreed; this basement was getting a little too claustrophobic for me.

The muffled noise was close enough to where Tony could hear, so we waited at the top of the stairs, but before the door even opened, we flew back slamming into the floor.

Tony landed on top of me, jamming his right elbow into my right side. With Tony's help, I got out the way as someone stormed down the steps.

It was Mrs. Palmer and the scary man. I asked Mrs. Palmer, "What's going on?" Ignoring my question, she checked Tony's bruised shoulder and said, "Thank you, Bynder," then left.

Bynder was another name on a folder grouped with ours. He stayed behind, eyeing us coldly, as if there was no emotional attachment behind them, as in not family. He stood guard, towering over us.

He would have been okay looking if it were not for that scar across his face. He had wavy hair and chiseled features that gave him a hard, distinctive look.

We waited patiently, not saying a word, waiting on any reason to break out. Opportunity knocked when I heard someone coming to the door. I told Tony to get ready. We made a dash for the exit as Bynder turned to see who it was.

As soon as I made it to the bottom step, a voice resonated in my head, stopping me cold… *I know you want to leave, Connor, but please stay awhile so we can give you the answers you so desperately want…* Shutting my eyes, I grabbed my head. Voice… loud… brain hurts.

I opened my eyes when I felt a hand on my head. A woman I had never seen before spoke to me. "Sorry, Connor, I did not mean to startle you.

Initially, my voice can be a bit overwhelming," she said, smiling down at me like my favorite kindergarten teacher used to do, and I found myself smiling back at her. She extended her arm toward the couch; I followed her lead and sat back down. How did she do that?

"You okay?" Tony asked me as I sat back down next to him.

"She spoke to me in my head, my head," I said.

"You did too when you told me to get ready." I looked at him strangely.

Willow, Byron, and Cheyenne must have been right behind her because there they sat cool, calm, and collected on the other couch. Must be nice.

"Now that everyone is seated, we can discuss why you all were brought here. My name is Tanzia, and it is crucial that you let me speak before you ask questions," said the woman who spoke to me.

Chapter 23

Tanzia was a petite woman with long dreadlocks that coiled like silk. Her hazel eyes were striking against her skin tone. She was very pretty, and from the looks of it, the guys thought so too. Their eyes stayed glued to her while she spoke.

With her, now stood five others, two women and three men, some of which I had never seen before. I only recognized Mrs. Palmer and Mr. Johnston, a.k.a. Shak, besides Bynder.

"There are those of you that will recognize us under different names, and there is a reason for that. We know that you are now aware of your abilities, and it is time to come forth and explain how you have come to be. I, with the help of my friends, will explain what we can," Tanzia said.

"You are a part of a race called the *San* (saun). Your kind predates humans that have come to evolve and has lived quietly on Earth thereafter for centuries, fitting in with these beings without abilities."

"We six who stand before you are your *Keepers*, each paired to you: Khan to Byron, Bynder to Scott, Shak to Tony, Tochia to Cheyenne, Selene to Connor, and I to Willow. Respectfully, we *Keepers* are responsible for you all.

"I know you know us as your neighbors and not of these names, but we did that in order to make sure your fathers did not falter on their covenant. Our sole purpose is to watch over you, protect you, and when the time came, educate you on our ways, your abilities, and our language called *SanI* (saun-i)."

"Wait, what are you saying, that I'm not human? Because I am very much so. I don't understand this at all," Willow said, standing up, tears already streaming down her cheeks.

Tanzia didn't respond; she only turned to Bynder and Shak. They both nodded, ran upstairs, and went out the back door.

Outside I overheard a vehicle pull up, some swearing, a scuffle, then more swearing. I recognized the voice expressing the few choice words and was surprised they found him. Shortly after, three people entered the house unlike the original two who left.

Shak was in the lead, with Bynder behind him practically dragging Scott down the stairs. He had on the same clothes he wore in the fight, only now he wore a zip up over his shirt that had grass stains on it.

He pushed Scott in a chair and told him, "Stay. He was right where we suspected." Bynder had to stand next to him to keep knocking Scott back down in his seat every time he tried to stand up or get in his face. Once, he tried Tony, and Bynder had to knock them both down.

After about three tries, Bynder put some death grip on Scott's left shoulder preventing him from getting up and Scott looked pissed.

Tanzia continued as if there was no interruption. "No, actually you are human, but a different kind, special ones.

Every so many centuries or when the world turns dire, our kind is born again to protect it, keep it safe from harmful beings. I know this is a lot to grasp at once, but you have to admit that you must have sensed being different long before your abilities came to pass."

Willow sat back down, shaking her head, tears still falling. "I don't know what she is so upset about." Scott pointed toward Willow. "I have always known I was different. I'm freaking stoked about it. Normal is overrated and boring. So can I go now, Pops? I don't need anyone to tell me who I am." His question was directed at Bynder, who didn't share his humor, but who could tell? His facial expressions never change. Bynder walked away from Scott and stood by the others.

"Good to hear it, Scott, but, yes, you need to listen, and you will stay put," said another man I didn't recognize from behind Tanzia. He was shorter than the other two men, muscular, had dyed blond dreads that fell to the middle of back. The color of his hair made his brown eyes stand out. Scott said nothing else after the man gave him a look and just sat back down in the chair.

"Sorry, Tanzia, please continue," said the man.

"That is okay, Khan, thank you. You were all born sixteen years ago. The San have learned throughout time to reproduce at the same time, not only for protection purposes but survival reasons," Tanzia said.

"Wait," I said, "but I won't turn sixteen until next month, and protect ourselves from what?"

Tanzia hesitated for a split second before answering, "In time, we will explain all that we know."

Was that it? What a brush-off. I didn't push it, but I wasn't satisfied with that answer.

"Protect ourselves from beings that can harm us. They are out there, and they are hungry for the abilities we carry, especially our *credo* (cra-dou): masks, or you may call it invisible. We are the only beings born with it, and your presence is known to others.

"Unfortunately, we had a leak amongst our people, making it easy for outsiders to infiltrate. We fear it is none other than one who goes by the name Ronin.

"Ronin is young but smart, cunning, and psychotically, vindictively dangerous. He is strong and has become powerful under the leadership of one named Monlow," Tanzia said.

"Monlow is an Ether (eh-ther) God—named from where the planet he comes (Ether)—one who is worshiped by his people. He is a powerful force that thrives off revenge and loves to toy with his victims. He taught Ronin how to take others' powers, and for years, Ronin has managed a group of misfits of this 'time' under Monlow's rule. Don't underestimate them. They are ruthless and greedy. Just like humans hunger for money, they hunger for power," Tanzia continued.

"Why doesn't this Monlow character manage these misfits himself, and what did you mean by 'time'?" Tony asked.

"He cannot travel to this 'time' without us sensing him. The more power one has, the easier it is to track. 'Time' means a place other than here," Tanzia said.

"So how do you travel there?" Cheyenne asked.

"It's not just one place. It's different places and to get there, well, some call it a hole, a doorway, or a portal. Other 'times' are not safe for us. We are too wanted for various reasons," Tanzia said.

"Okay, wait, so you say he is vindictive—so why is he coming after us? We don't know him," I asked.

"It's too long of a story to get into right now, and there isn't enough time to answer all questions," Tanzia said.

I just shook my head, again with the brush-off.

"Marge, our elder, ordered us to gather you tonight by any means necessary after you discovered the secret room," Tanzia said.

Tony leaned in and whispered to me, "You were right about her. You said the way she came down those stairs, something was up with her." Then he asked aloud, "What exactly is an elder?"

"An elder sits on a council which governs our kind. They are our law. Marge is the local elder we report to, and she was not too happy with the way things transpired tonight," Tanzia answered.

"Whenever *yougow* (you-gow)—younglings, such as yourselves—come to carry their abilities, certain others can sense it, and the more you use them, the more it exposes you to harm, like the one you met tonight in the house, Connor. That being was not so nice. You isolated yourself, but thankfully, Shak and Bynder were there to help. They took care of things while the rest of us met with Marge."

"But that is our fault. We wanted—" Bynder cleared his throat. "Well, some of us wanted you to enjoy life a little longer, but there have been sightings of the *nunan* (nu-naun), the unnorm, nonhumans, lurking. Usually, our kind has time

238

to train the younglings, but unfortunately, not in this case. Sadly, you are defenseless."

She walked over and touched both Shak and Bynder. "It is their mission to help you hone your abilities, show you how to protect yourselves through instinct. You have no idea what you are capable of and how to enhance your *renads* (ray-nauds)—abilities."

Then she touched Khan. "He will educate you on the law, rules, and the underground community of our kind, our government, and that of other worlds."

Next, she touched the shoulders of this tiny little frame of a woman, who could have easily been Cheyenne's older sister, named Tochia, and Mrs. Palmer. "She, along with myself and Selene, will counsel you, teach you about your kind, and how to be in harmony with each other as to become one, also to enhance your *renads*, to sense danger, and to know what to do. It is all about instinct and mental strength."

"Wait, that day outside of school, I didn't think anyone could see me, but you did. I should have suspected you then, but I assumed I messed up," I said to Selene.

"You're right, Connor, you caught me off guard. Like Tanzia said, it is called *credo*, from the old language of *Sanl* translated in English. It means 'to mask oneself, fade, or disappear' and *credod* (cra-doud) which means 'to reveal.' Eventually, you will not have to say it—you will all be in accord. You will just know what to do. *Credo* is just one *renad* you should have in common besides your individual one," Selene said.

"Also, aside from the unbreakable bond you hold with each other and us, at times you will answer questions that the other didn't ask. You will feel for each other even when you are mad at the other, but most importantly, you will protect each other even when you don't know why," Selene said.

"I carry three *renads*," I said, not knowing if I pronounced it right. "What does that mean?"

"It depends on certain bloodlines that come from the *Thinan* (th-i-naun), meaning to be 'well-off,' or 'royalty', as you know it to be. It was expected from you and possibly two..." Tanzia lightly tapped Selene on the shoulder. "Well, that is what it means," Selene finished saying.

Okay, what just happened?

"Where are our biological parents, and why did they have to give us up?" Cheyenne asked, changing the subject.

Tanzia said, "All we know is they disappeared shortly after taking you to the orphanage. It was decided among the elders then that the best defense was to have you adopted by humans, without abilities, to hide you as securely as possible. Unfortunately, since our kind is dying out, we have to try ways of keeping our bloodlines safe."

"I don't believe you. You know more than what you're telling us. It's obvious you're hiding something. Where is Vincent?" I asked.

"I can only tell you what I know to be true," Tanzia answered calmly, but I caught the play on words. She may not know something for sure, but she definitely is aware of a lot.

"Wow, really. Well, can you tell me this—you mentioned earlier about our fathers. Why hadn't our parents told us any of this? I mean I understand maybe one or two, but none of our parents told us anything," Cheyenne asked.

"Yeah, what she said. My dad could've told me about his deal long time ago. I would've bounced, no problem," Scott said, cutting in.

"Only your fathers were involved, thanks to Byron's grandfather, Mr. Conway," Tanzia answered, facing only Cheyenne and Scott.

"So this 'the *San*' council was the organization that made my grandfather rich, wasn't it?" Byron asked.

"Yes, the elders went to him because he had many connections. He was known to never pass up a deal, especially one that's guaranteed.

The elders handpicked your families along with Mr. Conway's aid, so he and only he was given full disclosure. Each father was chosen due to his unfortunate circumstances at that time and knowingly swore to secrecy by any means necessary, meaning their lives. They knew nothing of your real history, and your mothers figured it was a normal adoption," Tanzia explained.

"Circumstances at that time, you mean like, I don't know, say they were blackmailed or something along those lines?" Tony asked.

"No, due to their unfortunate circumstances at that time. Your families needed help due to illnesses, death, things out of their control. They needed help, and, in return, helped you by keeping you safe. The money just meant you would be well cared for," Khan said.

"That explains what he meant by allowing evil in— the secret society involving my adoption," Byron said, sounding upset.

"After some time, Byron, your grandfather had known regret with the deal. We think that contributed to his unstable mental state today," Tanzia said.

"We're not the evil ones, your grandfather is," Willow said to Byron but stared straight ahead.

"That is enough for tonight. We know you will have a lot more questions, but it is getting late, and I know your parents will be missing you soon," Tanzia said, as if she just finished reading us a bedtime story but this was no tale.

So that's it. We go back and pretend we live in, what is now, fairytale land and all is right with the world when we lie to our family and friends. I must not have been the only one who felt that way because none of us moved. We sat there dumbfounded.

"How do you expect us to go back to being normal after this?" Tony asked first, then we attacked them with questions.

"Enough," Khan said. His voice radiated so loudly, we backed up. He took a deep breath. "This is not how we normally approach you, but we had no other choice. I know that was a lot, but due to the present circumstances, we did the best that we could with the options that lay before us.

"We are around even when you are not aware. We have doctors to falsify records, cops to discard reports, lawyers to get charges dropped, and so many others to help us watch over and protect you," Khan continued, slowly pacing with his hands behind his back.

"You, Scott, all those times you were arrested for fighting and injuring the other person so badly just to prove just how strong you were. Byron and Tony, how many broken bones have you collected at a sports activity that healed at an accelerated rate? Cheyenne and Willow, how many car and motorcycle stunts have you walked away from with the many vehicles your parents continuously buy you? Lastly, Connor, how many times have you scaled a tree, outswam almost anybody, and run so fast, it was questionable by your friends? Not to mention all the other acts you have all done that I could not begin to cover—it would take years.

"Who do you think covered things up? And believe me, there have been a lot. You six are the most rambunctious individuals probably in our history. We have been around, and you have seen us, have you not?" Taking another deep breath, he relaxed a bit and his voice softened. "It will not be easy, but it has been done in the past by others, and you will do it too. We are still here."

With that, he was done. I have never been so overwhelmingly exhausted in my life.

I said my good-byes to the others, and Tony said he would call me later. I was seriously looking forward to that phone call. I stayed behind lingering, waiting for Selene as she finished talking with the other *Keepers*.

Chapter 24

Selene and I stood in her kitchen after everyone had left and the dust had settled. "Tea?" she asked me, reaching into her cabinet. "I have soda or juice if you prefer."

"Bourbon, straight." I laughed but was seriously hoping.

"Do not lose that crazy sense of humor, kiddo, but no." Instead, she handed me a soda and a smile.

We headed out back to her deck. We sat for a little while, not talking, only relaxing. I had my arms wrapped around my knees, stargazing. I took some long deep breaths, trying to soak tonight in. So I'm not crazy after all. Someone was following me around—Selene.

Without turning my head, I broke the silence "My dad, huh? What exactly did they tell him? Did he ask questions? Why did he agree to this? Does he know that I will know one day?" I had so many unanswered questions running around in my head. I needed more than what they gave us tonight.

"He did it because your mom was very ill with a rare disease that was killing her. No approved medications worked, and he was out of options. Agreeing to this made experimental drugs and the best doctors available to them. Mr. Conway, being his boss, was aware of your mother's illness and approached him, knowing he would agree," Selene said.

My mom was sick. I never knew. They never told me. She was waiting for me to say something, but I could not manage to form any words, so I let her continue.

"Your father knew it was an illegal adoption, but when he was told it was to protect you from bad people, he learned to live with it. Listen, when you are desperate enough and more money than you can count is handed to you, most people do not ask questions. Your mother, who thought she could never have another child, accepted you with open arms. Your father is a good man, Connor. You need to find closure with this. He did what he had to do for the both of you, but you can never talk to him about any of this. Do you understand?" she asked.

She said a mouthful. My picture-perfect family was not so perfect after all. I didn't know what to think or feel, so I said yes and changed the subject.

"Will we become *Keepers* too?" I asked.

"If you chose it, but usually the council has plans for us all. Usually, *Keepers* come into this world first to prepare *yougows* who will grow into *Dianads* (dee-a-naud), meaning defender of this world, when all your abilities have come. There will be a lot of training."

"Great, cannot wait."

She laughed at me, then went to grab us some snacks. When she returned, I had to ask the million-dollar question, "There's no Mr. Palmer, is there? What do I call you?"

She sighed. "Selene, please. No, there has never been a Mr. Palmer. I have always told people he left me. After that, people abruptly change the subject. I am sure you have seen a certain *Keeper* here and assumed it was my husband."

"Khan," I said. "Why is it a secret?"

"We really do not have room for personal lives. It can get in the way. I see the way you and Tony look at each other." I was blushing hard. I really was not expecting this conversation to turn on me.

"You do not have to respond, but feelings can get you in trouble. It is best to settle down once the danger has ended for some time. Unfortunately, we do not get the luxuries as others do on this planet. Khan and I slowed things down considerably once you all were born. We have our duties, and they come before anything else."

I could tell by the way she talked this was a hard conversation. Never in a million years would I have imagined sitting here, talking to her like this. She seemed so easy to talk to; I had no clue who she really was. I feel so bad the way I acted toward her when she was only ever watching out for me since birth.

"So what am I supposed to do, wait another sixteen years to settle down and find Mr. Right? I'm not saying Tony is Mr. Right or anything, but I don't want to be old when it's time to settle down," I said.

A funny expression came across her face as if I made a joke, "I am over sixty, Connor," she said.

I spat my drink out, nearly choking on it. There was no way she was sixty. She easily looked like she was in her twenties. Her cocoa-colored skin was flawless, and she had the body of a goddess. How was that possible?

"We age gracefully and quite slowly. Our kind can live up to about two hundred years. The year our abilities come in is the only time we grow and develop rapidly. You never stop eating and talk about the growing pains, ouch. I don't miss it. We are considered adults when this occurs, usually around sixteen, not eighteen," she said, laughing at me, not sounding sympathetic at all.

"Well, I definitely eat like a horse, but no growth pains yet. Sounds like fun, yea."

"Be ready, Connor, by next year, you will have a body of a twenty-year-old, and it stays that way until you are over one hundred years or so. That's when we start aging. It is smart to wait until things are calmer before settling down. That is why we have our children at the same time and centuries apart as to not wander alone and things are calmer."

"Wait, are we supposed to pair up with each other or something? I like Tony, but like I said, I don't know if he is the one. I want to choose, you know?"

Now it was her turn to choke on her drink. "So do we. It just worked out that way this time. There are others out there for us, so don't worry. We cannot determine our young's sex, and if we could, we would not do so. Years ago, when things were different, it was said we had a true match or *Destiny*."

"What is a *Destiny*?" I asked.

"*Destiny* is the one your heart desires so powerfully you can lose all sense of truth." Her smile faded as she continued, "You both are drawn to each other, not just one of you, but you have no control over it. It's irrational love bordering on obsession." She stood up and walked to the side railing facing the woods in front of us.

"Centuries ago before my time, people felt lucky to find their *Destiny*. I know that may sound crazy, but we are a passionate kind, always hurtfully so. Now since the way of the world, things have changed so drastically for us, most of us would be happy just to find love."

"How do you know when you have found your *Destiny*?" I asked.

"You will know, but listen, Connor." She sat back down to face me. "Times have changed so severely that your *Destiny*, if one is out there, may not be the person they were meant to be, so you are better off finding a sensible match, the one that makes emotional sense or simply find one you will learn to love."

I wondered if she was talking from experience. "When you say learn..." but I realized she was not listening to me but to something else.

Her whole demeanor changed. Her face went tense; she moved to the edge of her seat. She appeared to be scoping out the backyard. I followed her gaze but saw or heard nothing. Behind her fence were the dreaded woods. Now knowing that things really go bump in the night, they seemed even scarier.

"Run toward your house," she snapped at me. Her eyes were slowly turning a misty brown-green mixture. I could actually see the change occur. With us, it just seemed to happened.

She grabbed my arm and lifted me up so fast, I didn't have time to react. "Run, girl. I will be right behind you." I hopped the side rail, running to my house. I sensed something close, and it felt angry, like the thing that was in the room with me tonight. I ran faster. I turned my head when something grabbed me and threw me across Selene's front yard. I landed on top of her rose-bushes. The thorns sliced me good, but I couldn't focus on that. I

needed to get up and take cover.

Selene came running from the other side of the house toward me, holding a blade of some kind. Her lip was bloody, and she had a slash across her chest. She came right at me, raised her hand in an upward motion. For a minute I thought she was about to attack me, but instead her hand went down hard into something I couldn't see, but I heard the squishy sound when she made contact.

The thing she stabbed revealed itself as it fell to the ground, dead. At least I'm hoping, since she cut its head clean off. It was the most gigantic creature I had ever seen. Its skin was a pasty purplish color, and it only had on a pair of pants, no shoes. He must have been about eight feet tall and made of pure muscle. His neck and hands were enormous, and his face was abnormally large. I jumped back as it started shrinking into a normal human-size male.

"Go inside your house and lock the door. I will come in a few," Selene said, shoving me.

"What are you going to do?" I was a wreck, but I didn't want to leave her by herself.

"Get rid of him now, hurry." She started dragging the body as I ran across the street at full speed.

Something hit me in the gut, propelling me down the street. I slammed into the sidewalk headfirst and bit my lip. I rolled over and puked my guts out. I had never been hit so hard in my life.

I finished puking, got up as quickly as possible but felt dizzy. Half woozy and nauseous, I headed toward my house again but only made it as far as my parents' car. I needed to stop for a minute. I was out of breath, and my head was pounding so badly, I wanted to puke again.

What was going on? Why can't I see it? This is insane. Get it together, Connor, you can do this. I peered over the car to see if I could spot it but stiffened when something breathed on my back. I sent it soaring into my neighbor's yard, and when I heard it hit the ground, I ran for my front door.

Halfway there it landed on my back, forcing me to the ground. It weighed a ton. I tried to concentrate and send it flying but was too miserable to focus. It was pulling and twisting my head back so far, pinning me with no way to free myself. I tried rolling and kicking my legs to get it off me, but it wouldn't budge. Uncontrollable tears of agony streamed down my face as it tried breaking me in half, but I dug my fingers into the ground for resistance.

Suddenly, instant relief washed over me. I rolled over and saw Bynder fighting with it. For some reason, I could see it now. Tony grabbed me up, and we ran into the house.

Selene came running up behind us and locked the door. "Sorry, there was another one. It attacked as I was getting rid of the first one."

As Bynder and the creature fought, the creature stumbled into the street, and a car hit it dead-on, not being able to see it. The car swerved, slamming it and his car into a light pole. After a few minutes, the man staggered out of the car and fell to his knees in the street. Slowly, the man got up and went over the creature, which by now was human looking. It was dead.

Bynder stayed with him to make sure he was all right, even though the man could not see him. Selene explained that for Bynder to appear suddenly when no one else was around, looks suspicious; plus we need not be associated with too many incidences. Too many incidences stir up too many questions from the authorities.

Selene and Tony were standing at the living room window, watching the commotion outside. I sat on the couch, waiting for the pain medication to kick in as they gave me the blow by blow.

Bynder slid inside the house when people started to gather around the body. As Selene walked over to Bynder, she stopped short. "Connor, go get cleaned up before your parents come home," She turned back to Bynder but caught herself. "Sorry, are you okay?"

"Trying to hold it together." I really didn't know how I felt. All I could think of was the pain in my back. Tony sat down on the couch next to me and put his arm around me for support.

It was a nice gesture, but I wanted to tell him his arm was uncomfortable, but he kept watching me, needing to do something, so I let his arm stay.

"Listen, I need you to hold it together a little longer." She bent down next to me. "Your parents will get wind of this, and they will come walking through that door any minute, so please get cleaned up before they get here."

"Come on, Connor, I will take you upstairs to get you cleaned up. I mean, help you, if you need it," Tony said, tripping over his words.

"Thank you for helping her, Tony," Selene said. Heading to the steps, I heard Bynder ask. "Selene,

what did you do with the other bodies?"

"They are in the basement. You will have to get rid of them later on tonight when no one is around."

As Tony and I headed for the stairs, I heard them discussing tonight's attacks and how things transpired. I swear I overheard him say something about a setup, but that is all I heard once I took my first step. The pain shot through me like bolts of lightning with each climb.

Tony stopped each time I grimaced. Being a tomboy as a kid, I fought so many kids in middle school and won a lot, now knowing why. My body has never taken a beating like this before. This is not recess kiddie stuff anymore; somehow I graduated and didn't remember getting an education.

We made it to my room, and as much as I loved my bed already, we bonded like never before as I lay across it now. It was the safest place on Earth, and it brought me so much happiness. Tony took it upon himself to search for some clothes for me to change into since I was no help. He kept asking me what to put on, but all I wanted were my pajamas and my pillow, but I needed to get up to face my parents when they came home.

"How about this outfit?" he asked for the tenth time. He was trying to be strong, but I knew he was upset that he wasn't there to help me. In his head, I somehow became his responsibility, but I'm not.

I sat up to talk to him. "Whatever is okay with me. Listen, Tony, you don't have to worry about me I am fine, honest." He knew I was lying, but isn't that what you are supposed to say? "Stop beating yourself up because you were not there to protect me, it's not your job."

He sat next to me on the bed, sounding angrier than I thought. "I wish we were there or sensed something, you know. We left, and then those things jumped you girls. That's not right. I'm sure they waited for us to leave, then pounced first chance."

"Okay, let's clarify the 'girls' part. Neither Selene nor I have been a girl for some time, especially her."

"What does that mean?"

I shook my head. "I will explain later. Selene did a good job on her own. I certainly wasn't any help. We do need training in the worst way. You should have seen her. She handled two of those huge things with no problem. I felt helpless and weak." That was a feeling I don't ever want to feel again.

"I didn't mean anything by saying 'girls.' I'm just saying it wasn't a fair fight, that's all. Don't beat yourself up. None of us would have done any better. And you're not weak, Connor, you're one of the strongest people I know. Since you came into the group, we have discovered things in that short amount of time compared to the months without you. Plus, taking on Scott, and we know what he is capable of, you walked away with barely a scratch."

I doubted that, but I know he was trying to make me feel better. "Thanks, Tony." I gave him a hug, then went to go clean up.

"I will wait for you here," Tony said as I left the room.

The pain medication was finally kicking in. I set my things on the bathroom counter and turned on the shower.

I checked myself in the mirror, which was a frightening sight. My skin was ashen colored. My lip was bloody from when I bit down on it slamming into the sidewalk. My back had bruises on it from left to right. There were cuts on my front, back, and legs. There was so much wear and tear on me, I looked like a Dalmatian, and I didn't even remember collecting them all. No wonder I was hurting so badly.

When the bathroom filled with steam, I stepped into the shower. The water stung at first but eventually became comforting. I sat down in the tub, hugging my knees, soaking in the water.

I must have reached my fill of emotions because the dam of tears broke through and rained down on me. I thought about the adoption, my parents never telling me the truth, creatures trying to kill us—the list went on.

I don't know how much time had passed, but I got it together and started showering. My mom always said, "Every once in a while, a good cry is needed in order to move forward." She was right. I felt better.

Washing my hair, I found dirt and grass hiding in it. There was even a red piece of something in it, gross. I always had a head full of wild curly hair. I never liked it growing up, especially since Ebony had controlled wavy hair with natural highlights, she claims, whatever. I have grown to appreciate its wildness because it's like me— different. I like it even more now, especially knowing I can hide things in it. Got to look at the perks, right?

There was a knock at the door. "Yeah?"

"Hurry up, Connor, your parents are headed this way." It was Tony. How could he possibly know that?

"Selene got word," Tony said.

Now that's just creepy but Tanzia did say we will answer questions without being asked. "Okay, I'm almost done."

Finishing up, I hopped out, dressed quickly, slapped some gel in my hair, and pulled it into a ponytail. I even put on some of Ebony's cover-up so my parents won't see my battered face. As far as my lip, I will come up with some excuse.

Running out the bathroom, I heard everyone downstairs. I threw my dirty clothes in the hamper and headed down, but my dad met me on the stairs.

He grabbed me up so tightly, nearly squeezing the life out of me. It hurt, but I bore it because I needed every bit of it. I wanted to cry and tell him I knew everything and that he could trust me with it. That I'm not mad at him and it's okay, but I didn't. I wanted to remain his little girl for just a while longer. I don't care what any stupid paper says or how we came to be; he is my dad, and this is my family.

Holding back the tears, I pulled away from him, acting as if I had no clue. "Dad, what's up?"

I felt frozen in time as his face held that expression he every so often gave me, the one where words were never spoken. It wasn't a particularly odd expression really, but it stood out in my mind because he only shared it with me. All these years, I never knew what it meant, but now I know. It was the burden of my truth and the secrets not his to tell. He must have always been so torn between his untold lies and worried about my safety, our safety. My truth must have weighed on him throughout the years, and for that, Dad, I am truly sorry.

"Dad?"

"Oh nothing, doll face. We heard about the commotion outside in front of the house and were concerned..." He snapped out of it and became the strict dad I knew him to be. "Hey, you didn't call us like you said you would when you made it in, remember? What happened to your lip?" "Sorry, but as you can see I'm fine. Oh nothing, you know how clumsy I am," I said, smiling back at him,

hoping he believed me, back to the norm, right?

"You look sick. Are you sure you're okay?" he asked, checking me out.

I swallowed hard and held back new tears. I hate it when someone asks if you are okay when you're on the verge of tears. It makes the tears want to pour. "Yeah, just a little tired, but I'm okay." Honestly, I had no other choice.

Chapter 25

My dad and I headed down to the living room where my mom was thanking Selene for checking in on me.

"I know she is a teen, but they are not as grown as they would like to believe," I heard my mom telling Selene.

"No problem at all. I saw the lights were on and wanted to check on her," Selene said.

I stood next to my mom who pulled me close to her. I didn't see Tony or Bynder around. I listened out and heard them in my backyard talking. Bynder sounded stressed but had a feeling that was the norm for him. I excused myself and went to go check on things.

I spotted Tony, leaning against the gazebo, watching Bynder pacing while on the phone. "What's going on?" I asked when I reached Tony.

"He can't reach Khan. Everyone else is accounted for except Khan and Byron. He has called everyone to warn them about the attack, but now he is calling around everywhere to see if anyone had heard from him."

"So does he think Khan and Byron were attacked too?" I asked, getting worried.

"He didn't say but I would," Tony said. "Khan was supposed to make sure Byron made it in after he dropped everyone off, then check in like always, but he didn't."

"I'm sure they are all right. Hey, why did you two come back to Selene's tonight?" I asked.

"Bynder had business out here, so that is why Shak took Scott home and Bynder followed me. We were outside my house talking when he picked up on something and raced back here."

I was about to say something when I heard my mom. "Connor, are you out here?" She will be on worrywart mode for a while. I told him, "Let me see what she wants and try to hurry up as soon as possible."

"What were you doing out there, honey? Just stay close, okay."

"Where's Dad? Did he go to pick up Kane?" I asked. "No, he is going to spend the night at the sitter's. He's playing with another kid she is sitting for. I'd rather him not come home to this commotion anyway. As for your dad, he is out front, being nosy as usual," she said, shaking her head, hugging me as we walked back in.

Selene, my mom, and I were in the kitchen waiting for a pot of tea to heat up and having girl talk. I was so anxious to find out what was going on, unlike Selene who sat there calmly. She was driving me nuts.

When my mom got up to get the pot, Selene whispered to me, "Relax or your mom is going to pick up on your behavior."

I looked at her as if she was speaking non-English. "Relax? Didn't you hear Khan is missing?" I asked.

"Yes, but we have *feelers* out," she said. "*Feelers*, what are *feelers*?" I asked.

"What you would call hunters, but they search for the missing by use of visions they receive from impressions.

That gives them a sense of all entities. Their senses are not limited like ours."

My mouth was open to respond, but before I could say anything else, my mom was back with the tea. She was busily pouring our tea for us when she asked, "What were you saying, honey?"

I rolled my eyes and shook my head at Selene who gave me a raised eyebrow. I took a deep breath before answering. "Nothing, Mom, just nothing," I said between my teeth.

My dad strolled into the kitchen with updates and gawked at the tea my mom offered, but his reaction was more like she offered him blood instead. "I'll pass. Tonight calls for something a little stronger." He poured that nasty brown liquid called liquor into a glass and continued with the updates.

I never really realized how adorably handsome he was with his curly black hair and long eyelashes like Kane. His eyes always lit up when he gets the scoop on something. He was tall and thin and had a habit of talking with his hands in his pockets. Is that why I like it when guys do that?

"So the driver claimed the man appeared out of nowhere. They did a sobriety test, and it was clean, from what I overheard. The car must have caused some major damage to his face because the dead man looked badly beaten and disfigured. The cops seemed suspicious of the driver, so they took him into custody, and that was it. I feel for the driver, I really do, but people need to slow down in a residential area," my dad was saying, now enthusiastically throwing in his version of the story.

As we were sitting there listening, I became utterly amazed as to how clueless my parents were to what was going on in the world, but how could they know? It was at this very moment I realized I need to protect my family. Protect them as they have always protected me.

We sat and talked for a while until finally it was time to part. As we walked Selene to the door, she stopped to give me a hug and whispered to meet her in my room ASAP.

Shortly after she left, I told my parents I was tired and wanted to go rest in my room, then I said my good nights.

Chapter 26

I found all three of them in my room. Bynder and Selene were having a heated discussion about something. They were speaking *Sanl*. It would sound kind of nice if they weren't shooting out the words at each other.

I turned on the TV for noise blockage, even though no one was around to hear. By now, my mom was probably having a glass of wine and unwinding. She doesn't like drinking in front of us. I guess it's a mom thing.

"What's going on?" I asked Tony, who was sitting on my bed, catching flies with his mouth open. Why do boys concentrate with their mouths open? It's so caveman like.

Tony shrugged. "Bynder got a call from someone, and Selene obviously didn't like something he said because check it," Tony said, pointing at them. "They have been at it ever since." He was now smiling and appeared to be engrossed as they went back and forth at each other. I don't know how long this had been going on, but someone needed to stop them, and being that Tony had not made a move to put a stop to it, I had to.

My left hand went up waving as I cautiously approached the war zone. "Hello, um, guys, time out, but what is going on, and what were those things tonight?" I asked, hoping they would not lash out on me for interrupting, but they are supposed to be the adults here.

They immediately stopped talking, stepping away from each other. Bynder had his back to us facing the window, while Selene tucked her hair behind her right ear and cleared her throat before answering. "Those things are called *wolers* (whoa-lers). They are hired guns someone paid to come find us and report to him or her."

Bynder turned around and rudely said, "Too bad for them they won't be able to report to him, I am sure of it." Aware we came late in the game, but I was betting that comment was for Selene. The tension in the room was so thick, you could almost choke on it. I again cautiously said, "Okay. That's good to know." Not even coping yet with the reason they are unable to report. "Why did they look like that, and what did they want?" I asked.

Selene glared at Bynder for a second, then turned away, not paying Tony and me any attention. She sat down on my window seat in front of my bay window and stared out into the night, disassociating herself from us.

Bynder waited to see if she was going to continue and, after realizing she wasn't, answered instead, "They are paid guns, half giant, half human. They move exceptionally fast so they are hard to see at first. They are bounty hunters, dirty cops, or boxers by trade. They were given our location, and waited until we dispersed, then attacked. They are good hunters, but not always reliable. Being greedy creatures such as they are, one saw an opportunity and took it. First at the Caring House, and yes, you all could have died. Connor, you first if we didn't get to the room soon enough. I know you sensed something was wrong, but you chose to ignore your instincts," Bynder said.

"Wait one of those things was in the room with me tonight? Why did they attack again after you stopped them?" I asked, chills running down my spine.

"They usually work in groups. Most likely one went rogue and decided to attack at the Caring House without orders. The others probably figured that if they captured Selene too, they could sell her for a bounty, while capturing you as planned. Connor, whoever hired them wanted your abilities. It was a dumb move on their part because they walked away with nothing, not even their lives. No one ever accused them of being bright," Bynder explained.

"They may not be bright, but they sure are strong, and I have the bruises to show it, see," I said jokingly, trying to lighten the mood. That was a no-go. Tony gave me an "are you kidding me" face. You know, the one where you look gassy.

"I find it too coincidental that they went after you again tonight, Connor, right after you confirmed carrying three *renads*, one more than normal. It is not rare, but it does make you special, signifying your bloodline," Bynder said.

I wanted to ask what Selene meant by royalty earlier tonight, but she interrupted, "It is not what you think. There is no proof."

"Do we really need more proof, Selene? We all have sensed it, and as much as you want to deny it, you have to admit you have felt it too," Bynder said.

They said nothing, standing there facing each other. This was crazy bizarre. I gathered he didn't trust someone as she did, and I had a feeling that person was Khan. We waited it out, but once again, with no help from Tony, I elbowed him.

"So we are in danger then?" Tony asked, stating the obvious. Now it was my turn to give him a "really" face.

"Yes, you are, all of you. When the one who hired them does not hear back from them soon, they will send more.

That is why it is imperative we teach all of you how to hone in on all your skills. Although I have a feeling we may not get the chance," Bynder said.

Did he really need to look at me when he said that? Give me a break. I did my best tonight. What did he mean, not get a chance?

"What is going on with Khan?" I felt for Selene, but we need to know what.

"We do not know yet. We have *feelers* out, and hopefully they will get back to us soon," Selene said, and that was it for the night.

They told us they would take turns keeping watch tonight. Apparently, we're not supposed to need that much sleep, especially the older we get. I so don't agree with that one.

"Good night," Bynder said, nodding his head, then jumped out of my second-story window. Tony and I ran to the window right as he landed on his feet like a cat. He surveyed the area first, then took off, running exceptionally fast, not like Byron fast, but fast enough.

Tony looked back at Selene. "Can we really do that?" Selene smiled for the first time in a while tonight, then

said, "Yes, but I would not advise it at this time." Her smile faded as she looked at me, and I knew exactly what she was thinking. "Be careful and try not to get too close," I would have if only it weren't too late.

"Thank you, Selene, for tonight. I wouldn't be here if it were not for you," I said.

She grabbed both my hands. "Well, I am glad I was there for you as I always have been and always tend to." She squeezed my hands, then turned to Tony. "Good night, Tony," she said, then she too jumped out the window, taking off, running right as she landed. How cool was that.

I grabbed a big blue pillow off the floor, sat cross-legged on the edge of my bed, and sighed for the umpteenth time tonight. Tony fell into a wicker chair off in the corner.

"All these years I thought Selene was this nosy neighbor always getting me into trouble. Little did I know she was trying to keep me from getting into trouble." I slumped back onto my bed, gazing at the stars my dad and I had put on my ceiling when I was a kid. So many years had passed since then, but they still glowed brightly in the dark, one of the few things in my life that had remained unchanged.

"I know Shak worked hard keeping me out of trouble because, man, when I think back, my boys would always say I had a guardian angel. If they only knew," Tony said, tossing a pillow in the air. From the smirk on his face, I could tell he was thinking of some near-miss incident and seemed pleased with himself.

I was going to ask but then decided not to. Some things are best kept secret, or I would have to divulge some things like pulling the fire alarm in school, accidentally damaging neighbors' properties, and so much more, but we don't want to go there. What can I say? I was a feisty kid.

I stretched out on my bed, yawning a little too loudly. Okay, it sounded more like a lion's roar. Tony cleared his throat to remind me of his existence. "What are you looking at? I'm tired," I said.

He said nothing as he squirmed in the chair that suddenly became uncomfortable. I watched him awhile, then slid over only after I felt as if he was tortured enough. "Don't get used to this."

He strolled over, taking his time; he was so full of it. He lay on his back with his hands behind his head and asked, "What do you think about tonight?"

I rolled over to my side, head on my pillow to look at him. "Which part, the meeting or the 'wolers' attack?"

He turned his head to face me. "Either, shoot, both." "I was scared and pissed at first being held captive,

then amazed at what we are, and that there are others out there who want to harm us. Shocked to find out my boring dad is a part of a secret society that paid him to adopt me. Also, what's up with my age and the fact they didn't seem to want to discuss certain topics?" I really didn't think I had that much to say, but it all rushed out.

"Don't hold back now." He laughed. "Seriously though, I kind of felt that way too, except age and the scared part. I don't get scared."

"Oh, whatever, you so were. You hardly said anything tonight. What's with that?" I asked.

"Nothing. Unlike most people, I like to listen first, then let it all sink in. It's how my mind works. You common folk can't understand that," he said.

I punched him in his arm, but I think I did more damage to my hand. He finally admitted he was pissed at first, then thrown off about the whole situation.

We joked around, allowing ourselves to forget our new responsibilities, the harmful things we are now aware of, and the accountability of our actions that lay outside these four walls for a brief moment. We allowed ourselves to be everyday, ordinary teens.

There was a bang at the door then *swoosh,* the door swung open. I didn't have time to flinch before Ebony stormed in. "Who are you talking to in here?" I was so busted.

I glanced to my right where Tony lay, but she couldn't see him. Good reflexes. "What do you want, and don't you know how to knock? This is my room, you know," I said, pissed that she walked in uninvited. "I thought vampires had to be invited in." I love vampires but she doesn't, and she hates it when I call her one.

"Don't play dumb. I know I heard a male voice." She stood there in her unflattering putrid-pink pajamas with her arms folded waiting for an answer. If only Robert could see her now. She had curlers in her hair and pimple cream on her chin. She looked like the Wicked Witch of the West. I take that back, she was uglier.

"It's the television." I shouted at her when she came over to look under the bed. Tony lay there on the bed, watching her. "Get out. What are you doing home so early anyway? Aren't you supposed to be sneaking in a few hours from now anyway?"

"You better not have had a boy in here. I'm only looking out for you, silly girl," she said, ransacking my closet. She's nuts. "Oh, yeah, and don't think I don't know you got me into trouble always whining about me lying as to why I get in so late."

"Oh please, you're only looking out for your reputation at school. Besides, last time I checked, I had parents you know, the ones you do lie to." I said standing on my bed. I hated her with a passion and wanted her out. Tony grabbed my leg, getting my attention. He pointed to my things lifting in the air, but Ebony was too busy in my closet to see. I shut up for a second, relaxed, letting my stuff fall back down. This is going to be so hard.

"Hey, hey, what's going on up here," my mom said, running in. Oh great, here came my parents. Tony jetted across the room as Ebony leaned against my bed and sat in the once unbearable chair, enjoying the whole show. I was so embarrassed. "We can hear you two all the way downstairs in the den."

Ebony told them I have a boy in my room. "Okay, okay, you two, knock it off. The both of you are acting like a bunch of three-year-olds," she said. "Now you know Connor doesn't have any male friends like that."

"Connor, get off your bed," my dad said, trying to talk over us, but we were going at it. Really, Dad, that's all you care about? Instead of helping me get this bug problem called Ebony out my room, he leaned against the wall with his arms folded, taking it all in. Ugh, guys.

"Geez, thanks, Mom, thanks," I said, my feelings hurt. "Well, do you, Connor?" my mom asked.

Rolling my eyes, I said, "Of course not, Mom."

"I'm telling you, Mom, she had a boy in her room. I heard him," Ebony said, still fighting her cause.

"Well, where is he, Ebony? Do you expect us to believe he jumped out the window?" My mom asked, unaware of that possibility.

"Can you tell her not to barge in next time?" I demanded, trying to remain calm.

"I said all right, Connor. Now go, Ebony, or no game for a week for you. And if you don't clean this room, no swim team next for you, Connor," she said. How unfair was that. Ebony came in and destroyed my room, but I have to clean it up. Who cares at this point, as long as she was gone.

I slammed the door and locked it. Utterly humiliated and still pissed, I started cleaning up, avoiding eye contact with Tony.

"Wow, and I thought my family was cracked. Your sister is no joke, and what was going on with her face?" Tony asked from the corner chair.

"She was just being Ebony, and she cannot help her face. She means well in her own twisted way, but she comes across all wrong. I don't even know how she has friends. Sorry about that, but you don't have to enjoy it so much."

"Don't be. I found it quite entertaining, especially when you stood on the bed. So how did it feel to finally reach five feet?" Was he seriously cracking jokes right now? "All that was missing was popcorn."

"Ha-ha, all right, let it go already." I cut him a look. "Okay, I will stop," he said, pretending he was zipping

his lips shut as he sat on my bed.

"Anyway, we were discussing life and the many possibilities it held," I said, still picking up the mess Ebony made.

"Jokes aside, you have to get a hold of your emotions, Connor. Remember the locker at school and the fight with Scott. Your telekinesis is obviously a direct line to your emotions. What if Ebony turned around and saw half your things floating? She would lose her mind. Could you blame her? If she flipped over you having a boy in your room…"

He was absolutely right, and I told him so when I sat down next to him. I have to control my emotions and think first. What if not only Ebony saw but my parents did too?

I rested my head on his shoulders and closed my eyes. We sat there for a minute. He eventually started stroking my hair causing my heart to race. I raised my head to face him, and we started kissing. The butterflies in my stomach were racing as fast as my heart, if not faster.

For some reason, he pulled away quickly and walked to the window, keeping his back to me. "I can't do this with you. Not because I don't want to, but because I won't be able to stop myself," he said.

I sat there listening to him talk. In such a short time, I have come to care for him. We have done so much since we have known each other, but there is a lot going on. I thought back to what Selene said, "Feelings get in the way."

I walked over and stood next to him. I explained my feelings and what I thought about our... whatever you call it. Also, that advice Selene gave me and why, making sure to explain our aging process so he could understand it better.

I suggested maybe we should go out and do the normal thing like date, then see where it goes. He reluctantly agreed. I don't know why he was reluctant and didn't ask, but I was not ready for anything too hot and heavy. It feels like I'm already having adult emotions in a teen's body and unsure how to handle them yet. I guess that was a part of the change, but I already had a lot on my plate. We both did.

"I'm crazy about you, and I don't want to do anything to lose you, okay? Just remember that," Tony said. I heard him, and it felt good I had someone who not only knew me, but also is here for me as I am for him.

Chapter 27

I woke to a vibrating buzzing sound next to me. My eyes slightly opened to light, daylight, but I was still tired. I quickly closed them again and rolled over. Someone was shaking me and telling me to move over. I managed to open one eye and saw it was Tony, well, okay then. I must have fallen asleep while we were talking. I don't remember crashing or inviting him to stay.

"Connor, move over. It's probably my dad. I've got to get it." Oh, it was his phone disturbing my sleep. I said sorry, moved, then rolled over, drifting back to sleep.

He woke me up to explain. "It was my dad. He was upset I didn't tell him I was crashing out last night."

"Is everything okay?" I asked, hoping he wasn't in too much trouble.

"Yeah, he will be fine, but he wants me to head out soon to do some errand for him. It's just his excuse to get me home."

"Do you have to go now?" I asked.

"No, I have some time. It's still early," he said, crawling back into bed, making himself cozy. I was amazed how comfortable I was with him. If only my parents could see me now.

Sometime later, we woke to raised voices in the hallway. It was Ebony once again, voicing her opinion about something. Does she ever stop?

"What do you mean I can't go out because of some car accident last night, Dad?" Ebony said.

"I feel it's best that everyone stays in today, okay? It's rainy and nasty out. Besides, it's Sunday. Remember, we always had fun family Sundays?" My dad was trying to be understanding, but I knew he had his limits, and she usually found them.

"Yeah, Dad, when I was a kid," she said in her high-pitched annoying tone known as sarcasm. She was always difficult, only seventeen and already bitter. Where there no other rooms in this house they could have this conversation? Now it was time for Tony to roll out. I didn't want a repeat of last night's family dysfunctional playtime in front of him.

"Hey, I think it's about that time," I said, sitting up to yawn.

"That's fine. I need to head home anyway." He was already up, searching for his shoes.

"Sorry again about my family dispute last night," I said from the bed, watching him fumble around. He was clearly not a morning person either.

"Like I said, don't be. I enjoyed it." He was putting his sneakers on without untying them. Keeping his back to me, he asked, "Hey, you think it would be okay if I come back a little later, maybe around one?" As he said it, his tone was off, not the usual jovial one.

"Please don't tell me you are worried. I am fine," I said. "I'm sure you are, but I just want to make sure, and maybe I like hanging out with you, all right?" he said, hunched over, tying his shoes after he had already squeezed them on to avoid eye contact with me.

"Yes, I would like that," I said holding back any sarcastic remarks I so wanted to say.

"Besides, I'm not a 'love 'em and leave 'em' kind of guy," he said, then jumping out the window before I could toss a pillow at him.

I rushed over to peer out, hoping he didn't fall to his death. Just as I thought, he didn't execute it quite right. He lay sprawled out on the ground, not moving a muscle.

What an idiot, I thought, quoting one of my favorite female characters. Please tell me he didn't break his neck.

He slowly got up, checked his limbs, then limped off, smiling with two thumbs up. I had to laugh.

"What are you laughing at?" Ebony asked. I was laughing so hard tears ran down my face that I hadn't noticed Kane and Ebony watching me from my bedroom door.

Neither appeared happy. I figured it had something to do with fun family day. Like Kane has anywhere to go other than the backyard.

Ebony, on the other hand, never stayed home. I'm sure she hung with her cheerleading crew. I always and still feel they are a front for some sort of secret cult that lures little children to their master to eat.

I was in such good spirits I ran over and gave them both a hug at the same time.

"Hey, get off me," Ebony squealed as she wrinkled her nose, stepping back.

"Eeeww, you're a girl. Don't touch me," whined Kane, then I kissed him on the forehead. "What was that for?"

"You called me a girl for the first time today," I said.

"I meant alien head," he yelled, running off, pretending to shoot me with his toy gun as his dirty red cape flapped in the wind.

"Why are you in such a good mood, and what happened to your lip?" Ebony asked, sounding every bit the miserable being she strives to be. She focused only on my lip crinkling her face, touching hers. I'm sure she would die if she ever had a blemish on her face.

Trying to ignore her, I started cleaning up the mess she made last night as an excuse to walk away.

"Didn't you hear? We're on lockdown today, and what happened to your lip, I said," she repeated as if I didn't hear her the first time.

"I heard you loud and clear, Ebony, when you woke me up yelling from the hallway, and as for my lip, I tripped up the stairs, okay. Now let it go," I said, throwing stuff back into my closet, not caring where they landed.

"Well, I figured if we band together, we can change their minds. Make sure you cover up that lip," she said for the third time. She is so shallow sometimes, I could punch her face.

"Ebony, why can't you stay at home? Family day might actually turn out to be fun, and don't worry about my lip," I snapped at her for sucking my good spirits away.

Remembering what Tony said, I took some deep breaths to calm myself. "Why don't you invite Robert and the rest of the cult, I mean some friends over? Besides, it's raining out. We can throw on some comfortable clothes and play some games. It can be us against the old people," I said, smiling so hard my face was about to crack.

I could tell it was sinking in, but right before she agreed, she gave me an ultimatum. "Okay, but only if you invite your friend, you know, the one you don't have," she said with her arms folded.

"What friend?"

"Oh please, close your mouth, or flies will get in. You have been all smiles lately. I know you better than you think," she said.

I quickly shut my mouth. "Fine, he's coming around one," I said.

"I knew it. You little she-devil. I hope he's a cutie," she said as she hurried away. "I have got to call the gang."

If her voice could go just a wee bit higher, she would shatter glass. I ran to the bathroom to do a quick washup; the shower will come later. I was so hungry my stomach was eating itself, which has become the norm lately. It was Sunday morning, which meant some good cooking, Mama style.

Chapter 28

I ran down to see what was for breakfast. My mom made enough for an army. She already started making waffles, pancakes, bacon (my favorite ever), sausage, ham, and eggs with fresh-squeezed orange juice. Oh, how I love this woman.

I was beaming from ear to ear. "Geez, Mom, you sure went all out," I said, surveying the spread, salivating.

She popped her head out from inside a cabinet. "Oh hey, honey. Your sister said she had some friends coming over. You too, from what I gather," she said, eyeing me. That meant she expected some elaboration on my part as to who my company might be. Saying nothing, I walked over to the fridge to grab some juice.

"Is it Angie?" she asked.

Does the snooping into my life ever stop with this family? "No, Mom, it is a guy," I said, not believing I said it, but hey, she was going to find out eventually, like when he showed up.

"Oh, is it Tony, the one we met the other day? Is it getting serious? Because that's cool, no biggie." Her attempt to be laid back while trying to extract information out of me was comical.

"Golly gee, Mom, you should be a detective because your interrogation skills are very smooth."

She sucked her teeth at me. "Fine, I was just trying to make small talk. Just help me with breakfast, smarty pants," she said. "Ooohh, you're so fresh." She rambled on, throwing flour on me.

"You're so mature, Mom, real mature." We went back and forth, tossing the flour at each other when Kane came in with my dad, wanting to help.

They got to work, and before we knew it, Ebony had joined in, shocker. Yesterday's events seemed to melt away. This was the family I knew and loved. Okay, that was corny, but so am I.

The doorbell rang, and that was my cue to run up and take a shower. First, I called Angie and invited her to come over, who was all for it. Sadly, Hope was away on some family retreat this weekend, getting rained on. Better her than me.

Before hopping in the shower, I noticed my lip virtually healed, and most of my bruises were gone just since last night. Now that I can live with.

After the best shower in the world, I headed back down to a kitchen full of people I knew from school. That included half the cheerleading squad and the football team. Okay, maybe only a few people but didn't expect that many.

They were taking up the kitchen and the dining room. My mom loved every bit of it though, and it showed on her face because she was grinning from ear to ear. She always wanted a big family, although my dad put a stop to that. Besides the loudness, all you heard was clinking plates and "More please."

Tony, Angie, and Bobby didn't even see me; they were knee-deep into some good home-cooked food like I'm about to be in two seconds flat.

"Hey, honey, come on in before the food is gone," my mom said loudly over the noise in the kitchen. She was dishing out more food to the wolves.

"I see that." There were only scraps of food left. I was disappointed, but worst of all, the bacon was gone, all gone. A dark cloud engulfed my heart, causing me to sink into a hole of despair; my body felt cold, numb—well, until my mom pulled more food from the oven and the microwave. The cloud dissipated, my body warmed up, and all was right with the world again. I told you, I love me some bacon.

"I love you, Mom," I said, eyeing the fresh bacon. I grabbed a plate, filled it up, was accepted by the pack, and dug in.

We were all stuffed and the kitchen was a mess, but my parents came to the rescue. "Don't you worry, guys, your dad and I have it," Ebony, Kane, and I made a mad dash for the den. You don't have to tell us twice. I pushed Ebony and shoved Kane out the way. Ooops.

We set up the games, divided into teams of girls versus boys. The girls ruled, of course. There was fun, more food, and a lot of laughter plus some major cheating going on.

Ebony even gave me a wink of approval regarding Tony. I nearly fell out of my seat, one for the cheese factor of the wink and two for the approval. It turned out to be a fun day even for Ebony. Who is she kidding, she is a little geekette at heart too.

I was sitting on the edge of the couch when a sharp wrenching pain stabbed my stomach. I eyed Tony who was watching me. He was squinting as he squeezed his temples. Something was wrong, terribly wrong.

"Connor, Connor, I know you can hear me, and I know Tony is with you. You two need to find an excuse to leave, now. Meet me around the corner," It was Selene, and she sounded worried. "Hurry. I will be waiting in a black SUV."

I repeated what she said to Tony from across the room and hoped he got it. He hopped up, grabbed his phone, pretending to get a call. I guess he did.

He came back into the room. "Sorry, guys, something just came up, and I have to go. Connor, you want to take a ride?"

When I asked my parents, they nodded, waving me off, forgetting to ask any questions.

I ran upstairs and changed into some jeans and my favorite black Wonder Woman T-shirt. I hurried up and ran back down.

I yelled to my parents and Angie that I would call them later, but as expected, Angie gave me a puzzled look. I did the phone hand gesture, and she nodded. I was not feeling too guilty for leaving Angie behind; she spent most of her days here anyway. I will figure out what I will tell her later. She has a sixth sense about things, so it had better be good, but no time to think about that now. I met Tony by the door, then we left.

We hopped in Tony's car and parked it around the corner behind Selene's SUV to make it look like we took his car to go somewhere. She sped off as soon as we got in.

Chapter 29

Selene explained the physical pain we felt. "Your senses are *crand* (craund), heightened, now that you have come into your *renad,* so your body experiences it more intensely. In this case, I am sure you felt impending doom or trouble—the worse the situation, the more severe the physical manifestation."

Tony popped his head up front from the back. "What do you think is going on?"

"We are not fully sure yet. We do know that Byron is still missing and that no one has seen or spoken to him since late last night," Selene said.

"Didn't Bynder speak to him last night? No, I'm sure of it because Khan was following him home after he dropped Willow off," Tony said.

"Yes, en route to his house, but he never made it home. After last night's attack, we have to believe Connor and I was not the only target. We do know everyone else is fine," Selene said.

"So, zilch on Khan either?" I asked.

"No, nothing. Bynder has been trying all night." She swallowed hard when she answered, gripping the steering wheel tighter. She appeared calm, but I could tell it took all she had to hold it together. I hope Khan did not betray us for both her and our sake.

"Have the *feelers* discovered anything?" I asked.

"It's complicated, but their trail ended at Mr. Conway's house," Selene said.

"What's complicated, and what's a *feeler*? I never got to ask last night," Tony asked. I explained what a *feeler* was, what their purpose was, and that Bynder had them search for Khan last night. As far as the rest, I didn't know.

"We are regrouping in the woods at his house to figure out our next move," Selene explained.

"Our next move." She said it so matter of factly. This is all happening so fast, what has my life become? Connor, this is the real you, the one you always felt deep down inside, so embrace it. I took a deep breath to relax and told myself that whatever happens, happens.

We drove the rest of the way in silence except for the rain drumming on the car roof and cars splashing by. What would normally take a pleasant thirty-minute drive felt more like a three-hour paint-drying contest.

We went from seeing houses sitting side by side to open space of land surrounded by cast iron gates. The houses now were at least a mile apart from each other and set far back from the road.

Eventually, we pulled up to a remote road filled with gravel and dirt. If you blinked, you would have missed it. You definitely needed to know where you were going to find it.

About five miles in, we parked near some tree brush and walked the rest of the way through the woods. I normally love the rain but today, not so much. It felt cold, gloomy, and dismal, but I wasn't sure if that was from the weather or the circumstances.

The coolness of the wet leaves hanging from the trees stung as they hit me in the face. The little squirmy things in the ground decided to come out and play, enjoying nature's shower. I cannot believe after all I've been through, bugs still bother me, but they do.

The rain was turning into more of a mist the further we walked in due to the densely packed trees. We did not talk, just followed. It was quiet except for the rain's patter and the crunch of the leaves below our feet. The leaves were an array of yellow, green, and red, spreading across the ground like a blanket. How pretty it was, unlike our situation.

We stopped in front of a shed that had seen better days. It looked old like it sat abandoned for some time. Still, it provided adequate shelter for what we needed.

And this is how I came to stand in front of an abandoned shed not knowing what lay ahead. My life has changed so much but I have no choice but to accept it.

Walking in, Shak stood in the middle of the room, explaining some of what Tony and I already knew. Of course, Scott didn't show up. I'm not surprised.

"Great, everyone we expected is here. This is what we have gathered so far. After Khan and Byron went missing, Bynder put *feelers* out. They sensed Khan and Byron ended up here early this morning, but something went wrong. They sensed a grave impression upon this place. It is no longer a safe haven for our kind. We don't even know how Mr. Conway is doing or if he is still with us. So we told the *feelers* to stand down," Shak said.

"So what does this mean?" Tony asked Shak exactly what we all wanted to know.

"None of us *Keepers* can sense them, our kind. That means things have turned for the worse. We have unwelcome visitors here. This change occurred too rapidly, and only a few have the ability to manage that," Shak said.

"How is that possible not to sense them?" I asked "Some of us are taught certain magic but for defense

purposes only and not to be used in a manner of deceitfulness such as this. Khan was not one of those taught with me. He clearly acquired it under falsehearted methods. He will no doubt pay a grave price," Tanzia explained.

None of them showed any emotion, just rigidity. How are they so composed at a time like this? It must affect them, but you would never know it by their demeanor. Instead, they were all dressed in a plain black from head to boots, ready for combat like soldiers.

"So what about Byron, are you saying he's inside held captive or dead because that's not...," Willow asked, trailing off, staring at Shak.

This time Bynder answered. "Unfortunately, Willow, we cannot say. Bottom line it is up to us to investigate what is going on inside that house. I can promise you it is nothing you have ever seen before. We sheltered you for too long, but no more. No matter what we find in there and no matter what happens, we handle it. It is what we do."

"Anything for Byron, man," Tony said.

"I hope so because this is the best teaching you could ever have. Stay alert, stay smart, use your instincts, and never let your guard down," Bynder said.

"What should we expect inside?" Cheyenne asked. "Maybe we shouldn't go? I mean, us *yougows* may be

more of a hindrance than a help," Willow asked with a shaky voice, and her eyes practically bulging out their sockets. Now I actually wished Scott cared enough to show up. He may be a pain, but he could fight.

"We can only guess, but we won't know for sure until we investigate. You're better off with us inside than on your own outside. This here is how you learn to survive and the weak gets weeded out. I do not have to tell you we may all not make it out. Truthfully, we all won't," Bynder finished, and that was it.

Tanzia said something in *Sanl*, and the *Keepers* repeated it. Probably a ritual chant they do for times like these. A flow of energy passed through the room, filling it with serenity. I don't know how, but I felt more energized. The *Keepers'* eyes changed colors for a second, then back to normal. After that, we left.

It was wicked.

Jogging toward the house felt like an out-of-body experience. I knew my legs were moving, but I don't recall telling them to. For once, Willow made sense about us staying behind, but after last night, I really don't think we had a choice. I wanted to, no, I needed to, help.

I knew there was a lot more going on than what they told us. This felt more like a trap than a rescue, but this is what we do, right?

We made it to the house right as the rain started to pour. The back door was locked, and we didn't want to break it down, alerting anyone of our presence. Shak jumped up effortlessly and landed on the second-story ledge. He tried a few windows and finally found one that was open and crawled through. A minute later, he unlocked the back door.

We entered using the same back door Byron took us through the night we researched the basement. Once inside, Tanzia and I both listened to make sure we didn't hear anything or anyone close by. We agreed that no one seemed to be around or even home and expressed that to the others.

We had already discussed splitting into groups as soon as we left the shed. Bynder grouped with Tony, Tanzia, Willow, and Tochia, who would take the main level, while I grouped with Shak, Selene, and Cheyenne to cover the basement.

It was the oddest thing, heading down to the basement. We had to be careful since the cement stairs were damp or still wet even in some spots. The cast-iron railing was of no use if we needed support. It had rusted in certain areas, making it no longer safe to hold our weight.

The basement hallway seemed dimmer and narrower than before. The few lights that were on kept flickering on and off, threatening to go out. I needed to remove my jacket, since it was incredibly warm, not like the last time we were here. Maybe I didn't pay that close attention before. I was rushing to get it over with and annoyed with Cheyenne when we came, but I don't remember water on the stairs.

No, it's changed because there definitely wasn't an odor; it smelled more like pines trees. It was actually clean. Now, a smell of foulness hit me, and the deeper we went in, it reeked of mildew and rotten eggs.

I noticed brown stains on walls, small puddles of water on the floor, and cracked water pipes, forming brown puddles underneath them. It was odd that this much damage could have occurred in such a short period. How did this place get so bad?

Cheyenne and I kept shaking our heads in confusion and glancing at each other, stunned at the drastic changes. The once-beautiful, decor-filled rooms were a mess. All the furniture and decorations were stacked to the ceiling in each room and pushed off to the side.

I stopped to check out the damages, letting the others walk ahead of me. Once I got past the stench, I relaxed a bit after realizing things were not as scary as the *Keepers* made it out to be. Nobody was even here. Besides, Cheyenne could see through these rooms all by herself.

Chapter 30

I wandered into a room that had a huge wooden bookshelf made of mahogany. There were no lamps in the room, but the hall lamp provided enough lighting for me to see the design on the shelf. The carvings on it were so detailed; it was like nothing I had ever seen before.

On it were some old wilted books and dust most likely from the leaky ceiling. I grabbed a few books to see how bad the damage was.

"Don't you think they are keeping something from us?" "Geez, Cheyenne, make some noise next time," I said, nearly jumping out of my skin. I guess my nerves were on

edge more than I thought.

She leaned against the door folding her arms. "I thought you supposedly had superhearing or something like that, guess not," she said with that cold blank stare she so perfected.

"Well, I thought with your big bug eyes you should be able to see through this whole house, guess not," I said, slapping the book back on the shelf where I found it. Yes, they are totally hiding something from us, but then again she didn't know all of what I knew.

"Hate to interrupt your book and tea club session, but while you're in there swapping stories, something happened out here," Scott said appearing out of nowhere pointing down the hall.

"Where did you come from? I didn't see you at all. Not in any room," Cheyenne said, unfolding her arms, facing him.

"Don't worry about it. I'm here. Anyway, I was following behind Shak and Selene to see what they were up to because I'm betting you there is more going on than they say, when suddenly they just disappeared." I knew Scott was a little off, but disappeared? I gave him a blank stare as Cheyenne completely turned her back to him. "No, seriously, I was right behind them, well, a little ways, then they were gone. Like poof." He did some animated gesture with his hands and mouth, showing how something disappears.

Like I said before, he's crazy. Cheyenne rolled her eyes and walked off down the hall in the direction he was pointing. I followed suit, telling him to come on and show us exactly where they supposedly disappeared. They most likely just went into another room.

We caught up with Cheyenne, who was peering into each room from the hallway and shaking her head no when she didn't see them while I listened out. We searched and searched, heading toward the direction Scott came from just to make sure.

"I don't see them," she said.

"Yeah, I don't hear them either," I said.

"Yeah, well, I don't sense them, and believe me, my senses are keen," Scott said. He had a point; he was the one who scoped us all out before we knew anything about him.

"Come on. It was further back here." He started to trot down the hall where there were no more rooms and the hallway curved to the left then to the right. Stopping short, he pointed to a dark area down the hallway.

"Well, did you go down it?" I asked.

He sucked his teeth at me. "Yes, I did, but like I said, nothing. I walked down the hallway like this." We followed him. "Then bam, a wall." Sure enough, there stood a wall in the oddest place.

"Did you see or hear anything?" I asked.

"I heard a gush or something like that, then I peered out and nothing," Scott said.

"I don't see anything behind the wall. It looks black as in empty space," Cheyenne said with a puzzled expression on her face. I'm betting her face was a reflection of mine because I didn't hear anything at all behind the wall.

My spidey senses were definitely tingling. How do people just disappear like that?

"Assuming how big this place is, I'm pretty sure this hallway should go on for much further. Actually, this wall is new. See, look here," Scott said, pointing out a few discrepancies. "My ole man, my dad, does construction, and I help him out when he needs it or when I need the money. Anyway, the paint on this wall is a different shade from the original. Probably because that shade no longer exists. Also, the side panels on the wall don't match up to the main walls. Same goes for the floor tiles. This is crappy structuring."

"Okay, then why would someone build a wall here like this?" Cheyenne asked.

"I figure to keep someone from getting to the other side," Scott said.

"Or maybe it was built to keep someone in," I added. We stood there for a minute. "Guys, what if Byron, Khan, Selene, and Shak are behind this wall?" I asked.

"An old place like this has to have hidden passageways, how cool is that?" Scott asked.

"Yeah, sure," Cheyenne said, shaking her head. It was quite clear he annoyed her, but then again who doesn't? "What if the gushing sound you heard was a segment of this wall opening and closing like a hidden door?"

Without another word, we went to work, searching everywhere—loose floorboards, wall panels, even under rugs for a lever to open a passageway to the other side. We searched everywhere, even places that didn't make sense, like couches and pillows, until we exhausted all possibilities.

Then it clicked. I ran back down the hallway to the room with the mahogany bookcase, thinking back to the Caring House. In the room, I pulled on statues, books, pushed on more wall panels, but nothing happened.

"Connor."

"Yes," I said, turning around, but no one was there. It was quiet, too quiet. I no longer heard leaky pipes

or the lights making that humming noise, just quiet. My skin crawled with goose bumps. Something was wrong, terribly wrong. I slowly backed up to the wall behind me.

The room started to get cloudy, hazy like. I blinked a few times, thinking my eyes were playing tricks on me when the haze started to swirl together. It was slowly forming into some sort of shape right in front of me. I tried to move it, but I barely affected it. I tried again several more times, but it kept coming at me.

I ran toward the door, but the door slammed shut. It was too dark to see in the room. Something pinned me against the wall, squeezing my neck, lifting me off the floor. It was choking me.

I grabbed at it, trying to get it off, but I felt nothing but my own throat. I tried kicking my legs for leverage until I started to see spots. I was about to pass out.

I tried one last time to send it flying, and it worked. I fell to the floor, holding my throat, gasping for air.

I heard Scott and Cheyenne banging at the door, calling my name. "Connor, what's wrong? What's going on? Open up!" I heard them screaming.

I crawled to the door coughing, but I managed to turn the knob, but it wouldn't budge. I thought why won't they kick it in, and that is exactly what Scott finally did. He knocked the door off its hinges, grabbed me up, and carried me out the room. He sat me down in the hallway, and both of them starting asking me a million questions at once.

After I caught my breath, I told them why I ran back to the room. "I heard my name called then something started choking me. Next thing I knew, you two were banging and knocking down the door."

"Something, what do you mean something? Didn't you see it? It wasn't human? Didn't you see it?" Cheyenne asked.

Scott cupped her face. "Relax, I will take care of this." She knocked his hands away and pushed him out of her face. "You, what do you mean you're going to handle
this?" she said.

"Yes, me, since I'm the only one of us two that has managed to remain calm so far. At least Connor is calmer than you, and she almost had the life choked out of her," he said.

"This is insane. Connor said 'something,' not someone. What can you possibly do?" she asked, walking away from him.

"Listen, we said it before—they were hiding something from us, right? I have a feeling that whatever that was in there was only part of it, so don't let them think they really needed to hide the truth from us, okay? Besides, I'm pretty sure we are being watched," Scott said.

"You mean other than you, stalker boy?" Cheyenne said, grabbing his face this time.

Scott politely removed her hands, ignored her question, and instead said, "If you wanted me, all you had to do was ask." Then leaned in and kissed her, she backed away speechless. He may be off, but anyone who leaves her speechless is okay with me.

"Oh, by the way, Connor, I got your message to kick down the door, but next time, lead with that," Scott said.

I nodded. I hadn't even realized I did it. As far as people with abilities go, we needed to get it together. I need to get it together.

"I say after what just happened we get out of here, find the others, and let them know what is going on," I said. Cheyenne and Scott agreed. We are definitely being watched, and it's the same someone I have sensed all along, and it wasn't Selene.

Chapter 31

We headed in the opposite direction of where Selene and Shak disappeared, which should have been the way out. I felt bad about leaving them, but we needed to regroup.

On the way back, I could've overlooked it being dimmer because one or two lights went out as threatened, but I gained either some serious weight or the walls shifted. Maybe I was going insane, but I swear the hallway was even narrower than when we first got here. Before, two people could walk side by side; now only one person could.

The once bright yellow-colored walls covered in paintings had only stains with cracks, allowing small trickles of water to run down them, contributing to the thin sheet of water covering the basement floor.

The remaining four lights kept flickering on and off, barely giving us a steady stream of light to see. Coming in, I counted three lit rooms of the six we passed not an hour ago, but now there were only five rooms, and all of them were dark and empty except the last room going out, which would have been the second room we passed coming in. All the furniture sat piled up in this room neatly stacked. Strange. Now stood a wall where I swear the sixth room should be.

What did we get ourselves into?

I was about to mention it, but I stopped short, hitting the continuous wall extending from where the sixth room should be blocking our exit. "This hall should bear right instead of left, or am I just plain crazy right now?" I asked them both, pointing to the wall.

Scott pushed past me to feel the wall. "No, I clearly remember we turned left coming in, so now we should bear right to leave. We are supposed to go right."

"Maybe we didn't pay that close attention and we actually go left," Cheyenne said.

Is she nuts? "Snap out of it. There has been some significant remodeling going on down here in a matter of what, sixty minutes, and we didn't pay attention is the best you can come up with? We are supposed to go right," I said, beating the wall with both hands.

"Maybe you didn't pay as close attention as you thought you did, Connor," Cheyenne said, placing both of her hands on her hips.

"She's right, Cheyenne, it's like this place is continuously changing, like we're rats in a maze. Please don't act like you haven't noticed. Man, you're starting to act like weeping Willow," Scott said, waving her off, and as he turned his back to her, she punched him in his back.

"What the hell is that supposed to mean? What is so wrong with Willow?" Cheyenne asked.

"Girl!" He turned around, rubbing his back. "What was that for?" Scott asked.

"What's wrong with Willow?" she repeated her question. "Oh please, she acts all fragile like she is going to break.

She's weak, and you know it. How did abilities even get wasted on her anyway?" Scott said.

"Don't talk about her like that when you don't even know her. She may be a little sensitive, but at least she cares about people and doesn't act all hard like you," Cheyenne said.

They went back and forth, arguing and mocking the other. I couldn't believe these idiots. We were probably going to die down here, and they are actually arguing. And we're supposed to help others? Good luck with that.

I pinned them both to opposing walls neither able to move a limb. "Enough already. Just agree to disagree. Stop arguing and let's find a way out of here, or I will leave you both stuck to the wall."

Of all people to be trapped with, I luck up with these two. I wish they would just kill each other already, but the more I thought about it, I took it back. It's too creepy down here.

After they finally settled down, we decided there were two options: we either retrace our steps to see if things change back in our favor, or go left.

We opted left.

It was darker on this side, with only one wall-mounted light a ways down, and there was even less room to maneuver, so we had to walk a rigid straight line. Crushed velvet wallpaper lined the walls, and they smelled awful. Who came up with velvet anyway.

I'd never thought I would say this, but thank goodness for Cheyenne. She could see almost as well in the dark as she could in the light. So guess who led. She wasn't too happy about it, but she took one for the team. Did she really have a choice, especially after the way she acted back there? I was in the middle, and Scott was in the rear.

We took our time and kept our eyes and ears open. I accidentally bumped into the wall; it was hard to see, drenching my left arm, gross. The walls were wet, cold, and did I mention smelly?

It was quiet and uneventful so far except for the occasional drop of water landing on our heads. This side of the house was eerie, dark, and much cooler; and there were no rooms or doors on either side, just a long, wet purple wall that I swear was closing in on us.

"Stop," I whispered, slamming into Cheyenne when she came to a halt.

"What?" she asked.

"Shhh. I heard something," I said.

"Oh, come on, you guys. You're being paranoid," Scott said. "Is it me, or is it getting tighter in here, let's hurry up?"

"Paranoia for a reason, Mr. Big and Bad. Why don't you come up here and lead the way?" Cheyenne said.

"I would, but my eyes aren't as big as yours. They are like two big green lanterns," Scott said, egging her the same way as my brother loves to do to me.

"Really, how mature, Scott. Ignore him, Cheyenne. I don't hear anything anymore. Let's keep going."

I could see her eyes burrowing into him. What can I say, he did have a point—they are huge. That's what he meant by green lanterns. "Hey, Cheyenne, did you know your eyes glowed green?" I asked.

"No, and when this is over, Scott, you and me," Cheyenne said, turning back around. We crept on for a while without a peep, until I heard the sound again. I barely got out "Wait" when I slammed into Cheyenne for the second time.

"You really have to stop doing that," I said.

"You said wait, so I stopped. Don't get so close," Cheyenne said.

"There is only so much room in here, you know." I listened out, hoping I was just hearing things, but this time, I heard moaning coming from up ahead. "I hear noises ahead, guys. We have to go check it out."

"Why? I don't mean like, no, I mean like, I thought our objective here was to get out then find the others. Do we really think the others are down here? Trust me, if someone took them, they are in a place we won't be able to either get to or get out of. Simply put, it's a trap," Scott said.

"Even though it burns my soul to say it, I have to agree with Scott. We need to get out of here first," Cheyenne said. "Besides, the walls seem to be getting closer the further we move forward."

"We don't really know what happened to them, but if the roles were reversed, we would want them to come after us, right?" I asked. They were probably right and it may be a trap, but I had to go with my gut. "Listen, we came down here for a reason, so we need to see what's going on. For all we know, it is Shak and Selene stuck or tied up somewhere. No matter what, we handle it."

They hesitated but ultimately agreed. I navigated Cheyenne toward the noise, even though there was only one direction, straight ahead. I could see a faint light under a door ahead.

Cheyenne stopped, causing me to slam into her and Scott into me. "Cheyenne, now what?" I asked.

"You have got to stop doing that. The walls are squeezing in on us. My shoulders have been scraping the sides for a while," Scott said, ending his sentence with a rude comment or two.

"Well, it's not a vast amount of space up here either. I stopped because I hear something too. It sounds like it's coming from behind that door," Cheyenne said, pointing out a white door ahead. It provided a little light for those of us who don't see so well in the dark.

"Look, there's a clearing up ahead by the door." Scott shoved his way past us, but putting emphasis on smashing Cheyenne against the wall to take the lead. "Do you see anything?" he asked Cheyenne.

Cheyenne glared at Scott as if she wanted to kill him after shoving her out the way and soaking her back. As disgusted as I was that my back was a little wet, it was worth it to see how much it mortified Cheyenne. It was so funny, I went straight past laughing aloud to hysterically quivering from laughing internally. The tears ran down my face from sheer delight. I wanted to do a jig.

"No, nothing. It's black like I don't see anything at all, you idiot," she said with her fists balled, stepping into the small clearing by the white door.

"What, so your back got a little wet, get over it," Scott said, not apologizing or feeling an ounce of sympathy. "Oh, sorry, Connor."

I cut her off before another fight erupted and stepped in between them. "I still hear the noise though," I said, staring at the door.

"Well, we don't have a choice. If you haven't noticed, there is a wall ahead, straight ahead, and the hallway space on the way back is practically gone, so it's either door number 1, or we turn around and try and squeeze our way back through," Scott said, stating the obvious. "I don't know about you, but I choose door number 1."

There was no way I was going back. "Let's do this," I said.

Cheyenne looked back into the darkness and said, "Yes, but you know this is a trap, right?"

"True, but what other choice do we have? Okay, then I will go in first, and you two get

326

ready for whatever," Scott said, forming an im-promptu plan. We were fine with it. It was his turn to lead.

Scott turned the knob, and the door opened up on its own; it was inviting us in—not a good sign. The light coming from the room was blind-ing at first, so it took a couple seconds for our eyes to adjust, especially Cheyenne's eyes. Hers are more sensitive to light.

Scott took the lead, with us right behind him. The noise, whatever it was, had stopped. We didn't hear anything now.

The room was huge, and it actually felt warm and welcoming. The furniture was old, as in an-tique, but well kept. There were two deer heads mounted on the far wall and a gun rack with two hunting guns placed below them.

A bear throw rug was in front of a brown leather couch, a leather chair to the right of it, an old funeral painting hung on the wall above an unlit fireplace, huge wall bookshelves, which housed, possibly, thousands of books. There were more books on the floor and even on a table in the corner. The best were stairs that led to a wall-mounted bookshelf. It must have been a lifetime of books in here.

There wasn't a speck of dust anywhere. It smelled clean in here like lavender; total opposite of out there. This room didn't fit according to what was going on out there, just like that strange wall down the hall.

"This room is spotless. Who do you think this room is for?" Cheyenne asked me. "Byron's grandfather?"

"There is an open book, in the chair like someone had been recently reading it. I doubt it's his grandfather's. He can't even walk," I answered, still scanning the room.

"Where's Scott?" I asked.

"Over here, guys." Scott yelled from behind the wall of the mounted deer heads. Cheyenne and I exchanged looks wondering how he got behind the wall. We followed the wall until we saw a curtain in front of the bookshelf stairwell, leading to an adjoining room.

I was in so much awe over the bookshelf, I hadn't noticed the curtain. The curtained room only had a sink and a bookshelf that he was trying to move out the way.

"What are you doing?" Cheyenne asked.

"Look," he pointed to the floor. "There is a faint light coming from behind this wall. If I can just get to it…" He grunted as he pushed on it. It must have stood twelve feet tall and weighed a ton.

He managed to shove this humongous thing out of the way, and sure enough, there was a handle. It didn't look like a door at first glance, but there it was.

"Good eyes, Scott. A way out," I said. Things were finally looking up.

"I told you, guys, we needed to check out the noise," I said, relieved the so-called trap turned out to be exactly what we needed.

"I told you I would take care of this." Scott said. Cheyenne actually smiled. I didn't know she could do

that. I almost went into shock when she ran up to hug Scott, but even more mind-blowing, he let her.

Her smile was short-lived because things turned for the worse before we knew what was happening. First, I saw the expression on her face twist from happiness to sheer horror in a second, then I heard it, and without turning around, I knew this was going to be bad.

The next few minutes seemed like they were a blur. Cheyenne was still in Scott's arms, facing the opposite direction of us, staring right at it. As I was turning around, Cheyenne slowly let go of Scott who, at the same time, reached for the door. I don't even think he knew what was about to happen.

From my side view, I managed to see a glimpse of darkness before it tossed me across the room, slamming me into the sidewall. I heard Scott yell as he flew clear into the other room, slamming into the wall bookshelf, breaking it on impact. I don't know how many books fell on top of him. All I knew was what I heard, and I didn't hear him move.

I slowly got up to see where it was. Time no longer slowed when I saw Cheyenne suspended in midair inside a cloud of darkness. She kept grabbing at her throat and trying to cough. Her eyes flooded with tears as it suffocated her.

Not knowing what to do other than to help, I had to help. I had no clue as to what that thing was, but I did the only thing I could. I got up, concentrating hard to break the cloud apart.

It took a few tries before it worked but only for a brief moment. The cloud dispersed, dropping her to the floor, allowing her to catch a few seconds of breath.

It quickly engulfed Cheyenne again, suspending her back in midair. Then a segment of the cloud split off and shifted into fire in the shape of a man heading in my direction. It got hot in the room really fast. Before I could move out of the way, it punched me in my chest, sending me flying toward the back wall. I slammed headfirst, almost causing me to pass out.

Fighting unconsciousness and dizziness, I got up as the blazing figure reformed into the dark cloud. This time I tried both, trying to get into its head and knock it back. I assumed it had a mind because if it can do, then it can think.

I concentrated as hard as I could. This time, it took longer to break it apart. It was resisting me. My head was pounding inside when it dispersed again, dropping Cheyenne, but this time she lay motionless, not coughing for air.

I was on my own. It reappeared as a shadow in the shape of a man charging at me. It opened up what I think was the shape of a huge mouth screaming so loudly it knocked me back. It was the same noise I heard before, only intensified. It was an ear-splitting scream. I cupped my ears, falling against the wall, unable to block it. My head felt like it was going to split open, then it stopped.

Scott was up fighting with what looked like Cheyenne, but I knew it was not because there she was still on the floor, not moving. It had shifted into her form.

Scott was doing some damage to it, but when it got a hold of Scott, it tossed him around like he was nothing. The thing was just too quick, shifting as it fought, but then I noticed its movements had a pattern.

Following its pattern, I focused on its mind and screamed back, but inside its head. How does that feel? I thought it was over when it disappeared for about thirty seconds, but then it reappeared as me.

Oh, you have to be kidding me.

My head felt like it had knives in it, but I didn't care. I transferred my pain into it, causing it to buckle. Scott locked on to it, holding its arms, preventing it from shifting again.

This time, I sent a high-pitched, blood-curdling scream inside its head as I imagined ripping its body to shreds from the inside out. It worked. The solid pieces of me lay still on the floor, not moving.

That time I felt completely in control, mind and body. Scott and I picked up the pieces, threw them in the lit

fireplace, and as I picked myself up, I felt nothing.

Chapter 32

Scott grabbed Cheyenne, and I grabbed the door that led to stairs going up. We followed it until we reached a door at the top. Please let this be an out. I pressed my ear to the door, out of habit, but only heard silence. I opened it slowly to find an empty bedroom.

Not seeing anything move, I motioned for him to follow. I don't know how long we had been downstairs, but according to the window, it was dark out, so had to have been hours.

He placed Cheyenne, who was still alive, on the bed, then, like me, hit the floor. We were exhausted and looked a hot mess. Cheyenne had black smudges on her face and arms, Scott's back had bruises covering it and scrapes across his face, I had a scorched gut and bruises on my back, but were in one piece and we got out alive.

"Are you okay? Your nose is bleeding," he asked, me handing me a box of tissues.

My headache came back, but I didn't care. "Barely, but at least we are alive, right?" I said, wiping my nose with some tissues from the box he handed me.

"How about you?" I asked.

"I can't complain. Like you said, we're alive, right?" Scott said, smiling, playfully knocking into me.

"What do you think that thing was?" I asked.

"I don't know. My guess some sort of shape-shifter. Did it look like the thing that attacked you earlier?" Scott asked.

"Shape-shifter is what I thought too. That was insanely crazy. Those things are in movies, not real life. What else are they hiding from us, Scott, and why was it determined to get to Cheyenne?" I asked. "No, I don't know if that thing attacked me earlier. The room was too dark."

"I thought the same thing when whatever it was went after you. It could have easily gone after any one of us when we were alone searching, but it chose you. You're right—we don't have a clue, but I do plan on getting some answers. What I do know is that was sick what you did to it. What exactly did you do to it?" Scott said.

"I got inside its head, screamed like a wild banshee, and manipulated its organs to move into opposite directions. Don't ask me how I did it, I basically winged it," I explained to him. What I didn't tell him was it bothered me that I didn't care that I killed it.

"Keep winging it if it works for you. Listen, if I go search for the others, will you be okay watching her?"

"I think we should stick together, Scott, especially after what just happened," I said.

"I know, but I think she"—Scott pointed to Cheyenne—"should rest."

"If 'she' means me, then 'she' is okay. I can manage," Cheyenne said, sitting up.

Both of us turned around to check on her. "How do you feel? Can you walk?" We sat next to her on opposites sides of the bed.

"I am fine, just a little drained," Cheyenne said, rubbing her throat. "What was that thing? What happened?" We explained what happened to each of us, what we thought it was, and how we escaped. As Scott went into the details of the fight, I got up when I heard something.

I froze when I definitely knew I heard a noise from somewhere close by.

"What is it?" Cheyenne asked.

Walking toward the door, I whispered, "I hear voices, but they sound normal, as in human, you know." Both of them were behind me asking what they were saying.

"I hear a male voice. It sounds familiar but what if…" I started to say, trailing off as soon as I recognized the voice. It was Khan, and his voice sounded calm. I didn't know if that was a good thing or a bad thing.

He was talking to another man about demands, plans, or something like that. I couldn't exactly make it out because for some reason, it sounded muffled. This wasn't a good sign, Khan being so calm. He is supposed to be tied up somewhere screaming for help.

"Well, at least we know he's not hurt after all. Do you hear Byron or the others?" Cheyenne asked. "Wait, so if Khan is fine, then why hasn't he contacted anyone?"

"No, I don't recognize the other voice. Yeah, well, I guess Bynder was right about Khan after all," I said, leaning against the door.

Both of them looked at me as if to ask what. Remembering they were not in my room the night Bynder was hinting about Khan switching sides, I explained everything.

"So that's what they are hiding. I knew it had something to do directly with us," Scott said, referring to all of us, including the *Keepers*.

"I'm sure we haven't been informed of a lot more than just that. We are so in the dark about, well, everything," I said, but to make sure I understood Scott, I asked him to elaborate.

"If it were a matter of a simple kidnapping, then they would have gotten the police involved, right? If our kind or the *nunan* has lain low and followed the rules, blending in all this time, then why do we, all of us, need to take care of this particular situation?" Scott explained, pacing back and forth from the window to the bed.

"I'm thinking if one of them, meaning a *Keeper*, turned rogue, then we would have to get involved. Chances are if a *Keeper* switches sides, then it will be something crazy serious as in non-human involvement, like, uh, I don't know, that off-the-hook shape-shifter downstairs," Scott explained, plopping himself down on the bed.

"I can believe it. People make deals with the devil all the time. If Khan is walking around, he

is definitely involved. Besides, it's too coincidental how you and Selene were attacked right after
everyone left the meeting. How else would they
know where we were unless someone on the inside tipped them off?" Cheyenne said.

"See what I'm talking about. Oh yeah, I forgot
about the first attack for a minute. The more I
think about it, Connor, this has something to do
with you. I don't believe in coincidences. I believe
people just don't want to see the truth," Scott
added.

"Maybe, maybe not, but we can't make as-
sumptions until we get all the facts," I said.

"I hear you, guys, but we need to get out of
here. Now I hear the voices, which means they
are close, and we can't get answers if we're dead,"
Cheyenne whispered, making a very good point.

We tiptoed out the room, heading in the opposite direction of the voices. We walked down the
halls, checking the rooms as we went, hoping to
bump into the others.

Finally, I heard my name as soon as we
reached the end of the second hallway. *Connor,
turn right and wait for us we will meet you in the
hallway*, Tanzia said, so I mentally relayed the

message to Cheyenne and Scott. I figured that would be smarter.

We waited no more than three minutes before they came into view. They all were accounted for: Bynder, Tony, Tanzia, Willow, and Tochia. I had never been to so happy to see them in my life. Everyone, except Willow, had a few bruises, especially Bynder, who had his left hand bandaged besides a bloody shirt. We quickly rehashed what we all discovered and that Shak and Selene were missing. Tanzia explained they sensed that and there must be a barrier surrounding the others that's why we are unable to sense them. Ronin has let his presence known, allowing us to find him. He's inviting us to come to him.

"Do you understand the seriousness of the situation now, Scott," Bynder said not so much as a question but telling him.

"I'm here aren't I," Scott answered.

This time, we stayed together. There were so few of us left now, we didn't want to take any chances falling into another one of Ronin's unpredictable game of traps.

We were heading back down to the main level, since Tanzia felt a strong pull in that direction. Her senses seemed to be the strongest of the *Keepers.* I wonder why. Maybe if I make it out of here, that is definitely on the list of questions I need answered.

Do you sense him, Connor? Tanzia asked, walking beside me.

I knew exactly whom she was talking about but didn't fear him as I should. After meeting the *Keepers,* I tried to tell myself it was Selene, but deep down inside I knew it wasn't. Two years ago, he made his presence known to me, but I never told anyone, and I don't know why. I have never feared him, only felt safer knowing he was there, but tonight that was all going to change. *Yes,* I responded, but I didn't ask who. I didn't want to know, just not yet.

Be careful tonight, Connor. You are the strongest of the yougows. Use your instincts only, and don't let emotions affect you. He wants his revenge, Connor. He wants you.

I simply nodded.

As she walked up, surprisingly, Cheyenne and Willow came up on either side of me to grab my hands. It may have been in my head, but it helped. It was just what I needed.

We walked that way until we reached the stairs. As I descended the stairs, I couldn't help but think how we were purposely walking right into a trap for the second time tonight.

Chapter 33

We safely made it to the main level of the house, where it was calm except for a storm brewing outside. No one greeted us, only an empty living room but I knew whoever they were, they were close by. We stood around, spread out, waiting for the inevitable.

"Come out, Ronin, I know you are here!" shouted Tanzia, scanning the room.

In walked two males and two females who said nothing as they surrounded us. They were clearly not human and definitely scary looking, especially the females.

The guys each had spiked hair and dressed in leather clothing, their arms covered in tattoos.

I recognized the one female as the person we almost ran into the night we snuck in, and even though she had on a uniform, you could tell she could care less about anyone or anything. She was blonde, bug-eyed, and buff. The other female was questionable herself. She had the goth look down pat, but I really think that pasty color was real and not makeup.

Right after they were in position, a third man strolled in, carrying a staff, and all eyes were on him. My guess was this was Ronin. He was the tallest of them. He wore a black-and-dark-maroon leather jacket that stretched to the floor and slightly fitted black pants with black boots.

"You took so long, Tanzia. I thought you didn't recognize my voice anymore." His tone sounded upset, but his face showed he could care less. "Please wait, there is someone dying to see you again," he stressed the word "dying," clearly making his point.

He raised the black cane and struck the floor with it not twenty feet in front of us. The striking motion made a loud crackling sound, spontaneously creating electricity in the air.

It was such a strong surge that I started to walk toward it, but Tanzia physically stopped me.

A lightning bolt struck in the middle of the room, but it did not disappear like it should have; instead it lingered a while. It grew in size, opening up to form a big circular bright silver light. It sounded like a gush of water or wind similar to what Scott said he heard in the basement.

This had to be a portal to 'time', that unsafe place for us. Tochia yelled get back, but my legs locked. I didn't move. I needed to see up close who or what felt our lives were so expendable.

Out stepped a man, an extremely tall man, who wore a black suit and a top hat. He just stood there smiling at us. It was the strangest thing I had ever seen. He didn't look real. I slowly backed up to the others, wanting to get as far away as possible from him.

His aura was powerful, almost suffocatingly so. The light behind the tall man closed like a vacuum, and it was calm again in the room.

"Let me introduce myself to those who have not had the pleasure of meeting me. My name is Tanner." He bowed when he introduced himself, top hat in hand, like in a theater. He acted as if he was on stage, putting on a Broadway show.

Ronin tossed the man the black cane, then stood off to the side and leaned against the front wall eyeing me. "Thank you, Ronin." Tanner gestured toward the couch, smiling as if he wanted us to take a seat, like the show was about to begin any minute.

We just stood there ignoring his request, but rather observing him, strangely waiting for him to make a move. He pulled out three vials of something I could not make out, but this time insisted we take a seat.

Tochia tried to electrocute the man as he turned away for a brief second, but he was too fast for her.

Before the electricity could even get close to him, he moved out of the way, took one vial out, and threw it down on the floor, smashing into pieces. At first it seemed like nothing occurred, then Tochia dropped like dead weight, not moving.

As I reached for her, Tanner replied, "I would not do that if I were you. Even though I don't need a vial for you, I would love to punish your babysitters for your actions." I slowly moved back and sat down.

"If you're wondering what this is, young lady, it's my guarantee that your *Keepers* will behave. We can thank your oh-so-trusting *Keeper* Khan for these, te-he," he said, making a sound, which I could only guess was a laugh.

I asked Tanzia what was in the vials, but Tanner answered for her. "I can answer that, young lady. Oh, don't look so surprised. You have not learned to block your thoughts yet, so I hear you loud and clear," he said, staring at me with that bizarre smile on his face. "My goodness, Tanzia, what are you teaching these kids nowadays?"

"Get on with it, Tanner. We did not come here to sit around and watch you perform. Trust me, you are the only one amused," Bynder said.

"Well let me first explain to the girl," he said to Bynder then turned toward me. "These keepsakes are part potion and part *Keepers'* blood, your *Keepers'* blood to be exact, young lady, te-he. It, oh, how can I say this nicely, kills them."

Dead, Tochia is dead. Oh my god.

"I'm so glad you all could make it. I knew you could not resist tonight's performance." He clapped his hands and in walked Khan, practically dragging Byron into the room. Beside him was a man I'd never met before, but he was definitely human. The man's eyes stayed glued to Byron.

347

Khan sat Byron down in a chair next to us. Byron appeared to be in a trance. He just looked straight ahead, not blinking.

Khan would not make eye contact with any of us and kept his eyes on his destination only. Once he stood near Tanner, he snapped his fingers, and Byron came out of it.

Byron looked around groggily and asked, "What happened? How did I get here?"

Bynder told Byron to relax and that he was safe. He put a hand on his shoulder then he turned back to Tanner. "What do you want? You still Monlow's errand boy?"

The creepy smile faded from Tanner's face as he glared at Bynder. "Bynder, Bynder, Bynder, I see you're still babysitting, huh? Are things getting any better, or do you still hide out in the bushes and peep through little boys' windows at night?" And with that comment, the creepy smile was back. "It's not what I want, it's want I can do for you. We can make this easy or hard, but either way, I will get what I came for."

"Where are the others, Selene and Shak?" Bynder asked, ignoring his last comment.

"They are well hidden," Khan answered for Tanner.

Tanner glimpsed at him from the corner of his eyes when he spoke. "They are somewhere out of reach to you, but don't worry, they are in good hands." As he spoke, Tanner squeezed Khan's shoulder, causing him to wince. He tried to hide it, but it obviously hurt.

"You know what I love about you *Keepers*?" he asked, then stopped and gazed out at us with a dramatic pause. "You're all so weak and predictable, getting yourselves involved emotionally with these younglings. I found you quite disappointing and nonchallenging, honestly. Two of your kind go missing, and you run like a pack of dogs, scaling buildings and whatnot. Just the sight of you makes me sick. If it were up to me, I would dispose of you all."

He sucked his teeth in disgust, and his face changed into something monstrous, then he quickly turned his back to us.

The others with him became amped up, as if ready to attack. To me, they seemed more like the pack of rabid dogs. The only one who remained calm was Ronin.

"Call off your mutts now, or they won't be the only ones hurt, Tanner," Bynder demanded, standing up.

Tanner turned back around with that sick smile of his, clapped his hands twice, ordering the others to back off.

"Well, obviously it is not up to you since you still have a master, right? So what is Monlow up to now?" Bynder asked.

"Cute, real cute. He wants what we all want—power. As you well know, when your kind spits out a new batch of weaklings, we use them for either slaves or simply take their powers and dispose of them," Tanner said.

"Well, then what are you waiting for?" Tanzia said, standing up.

"Fine, so here are your options: either we take your powers, or you can simply hand them over. If you come with us, I can promise you that you will make it back here safely, powerless but safe," Tanner said.

"Dad," Byron said. "What are you doing here? What's going on?" he asked the man standing next to Khan. It was his father, Mr. Conway.

Mr. Conway attempted to walk over to him, but Khan put his arm up to stop him. "Listen, son, I know you won't understand this now, but I did this for our family's safety."

"What did you do?" Byron asked.

"These powers, gifts, whatever you want to call them, have only put you in danger for some time now, and no good can come from them. They are evil," Mr. Conway said.

Byron looked at him in disbelief. "You sound like Grandfather, but at least he's a sick old man, but you...

you have lied to me all my life, now this?"

"I know it looks bad, Byron, but I am only doing what's best for you, for us. I have made many sacrifices for this family, and I still am. You..." Mr. Conway's mouth was sewn shut. His eyes opened wide as he felt his mouth. He tried to continue talking, but all that came out were moaning sounds.

"Te-he, sorry, bored with the conversation," Tanner said, smiling at him.

"What did you think, you can trust something like him and walk away to talk about it?" Tanzia said to Mr. Conway, pointing at Tanner. "You get

351

what you deserve." Out the corner of my eye, I saw Tochia move. Not possible. In all the commotion, no one else seemed to have noticed. She was eyeing me, then Tanner, then back to me. At first, I didn't understand what she wanted, then it clicked. At least, I hoped it did.

"Well, here we are, young, inexperienced, and tired of your threats. So either bring it and lose or go back to where you came because I'm sick of listening to you blabber on about nothing," I said, swallowing hard, hoping I did the right thing.

One of the rabid dogs came at me, but Ronin chopped him in the throat. The guy went down.

Instead, Tanner walked down to me, not smiling anymore. With his hands clasped behind him, he gave me a once-over. I managed to look him straight in his eyes as he towered over me about three feet high. He smelled like raw sewage causing my stomach to churn. His face was dry, cracked, and his skin was truly ashen white.

"My, what a brave little soul are we. Don't let this smile fool you, little girl. The only reason you're still here is because I have my orders, mundane as they are," Tanner said. "I do recall saying that I don't need a vial on you, right, but never said that I didn't have one, did I? Insurance is always a necessity."

He held his hand out toward the others, and Ronin walked over to me and introduced himself. "You, I have been waiting a long time to meet."

My skin crawled at what he said, yet at the same time, he mesmerized me, his voice captivated me. He was the most beautiful creature I had ever laid eyes on. His face was so close to mine, I had to tell myself to breathe.

I had to make myself breathe.

Tanzia was right. He couldn't have been more than seventeen. His complexion was just a hint darker than sun kissed. He stood at least six feet tall with a slim muscular built. He had loose, curly jet-black hair that fell just about to his shoulders. His eyes were different colors, one brown, and the other green. They were the most striking images, even though behind them brewed hatred for me.

I wanted to, no, I needed to, reach out and touch him. What is wrong with me?

"You don't know just how special you are to me, just how important this night is for you. If you don't fight it and come back with me willingly, I will show you a far better time than that little boy did tonight. If you fight me, well, then I will only forcibly take you. Your choice."

"Back off, Ronin, this isn't even your fight. You don't know the truth," Bynder said standing next to me. His words sounded more like a plea. It was the most humane I'd ever heard him speak to anyone.

"Who are you to talk to me? Stay in your place, *Keeper*," Ronin spat, stepping into Bynder's face. His hands were balled into fists, ready to attack any minute.

I don't know why, but I stepped in between them. Ronin turned his attention back to me. His face and body softened for a minute as he stared at me, but for that brief minute, he allowed me to catch a hint of something else behind those eyes. That strong sense of familiarity washed over me, consuming me all at once.

My *Destiny*.

This living being, whoever, or whatever he was, was my *Destiny*. He is whom I have sensed shadowing me all this time. Ronin must have felt it too because his eyes squinted as shock flooded across his face. He quickly caught it, and his de-meanor hardened again, but he didn't look away.

Tanner leaned into Ronin and whispered to where only he and I could hear the words, "She is beautiful, isn't she? Just deliciously delightful. You cannot keep your eyes off of her, can you, Ronin?" Did Tanner know?

Ronin did not answer him, only gave him a vicious look, handed over the six vials told him to end this already and walked off. "Why, thank you. Always a pleasure doing business with you, sir," Tanner said to Ronin, who now stood with the others, no longer looking at me. I was disap-pointed and confused, but my world halted when I saw what Tanner held in his long white hands. How was that possible, vials of us? No one had taken any blood from me.

"You're bluffing. Those are not real," Bynder said. "Do you want to challenge me, Bynder?" Tanner

smirked.

He walked toward Bynder but stopped short. "I'm sure the person who acquired these for me would beg to differ." Then he turned to his other insider. "Right, Willow?" Tanner said, smiling at her.

Willow faced Byron first, already sobbing; she walked over to him. "I'm sorry, but your father came to me and begged me for my help. This is a messed-up world we live in, and I figured... I mean, oh please, talk to me."

She continued to cry, but Byron said nothing. He stared at her, expressionless. His body stiffened when she touched him, causing her to pull away. She looked at the rest of us, begging for understanding, but there was none to give. I felt my heart sink to my stomach. Scott was wrong—she was not only weak, but a traitor.

Tanzia took hold of Willow and walked her over to Khan, pushing her into him. "You made this mess, now you take care of it." Khan said nothing. He grabbed Willow by her arm and shoved her off to the side as she continued to cry.

Tony came over to stand by me but kept his eyes on Ronin, who was now staring at him. Ronin seemed more concerned with what Tony was doing than what was going on around us. At first, I didn't get why Tony came over, but he placed a pocket knife in my left hand. I got it—protection.

"As much as I enjoy this little show, we must be leaving. So, *Keepers*, what will it be? Either I take them, or you can simply sacrifice yourselves," Tanner asked.

Without a word, we huddled together, backs to the others. We were surrounded. Whatever will happen, then so be it.

Once Tanner saw our stance, he decided to break all vials, but nothing, not a thing happened, and from Willow's facial expression, she didn't expect it either.

Within a blink of an eye, a bolt of lightning sent Tanner flying to the back wall. Tochia was up and on him, not letting up, continuously electrocuting him.

The Chaos Began

It started simultaneously, and without a clue what we're up against, but we had no choice. Ronin attacked Bynder first, sending him sailing across the room. The nurse exhaled fire, engulfing Tanzia, who quickly responded within a protection barrier. Tony and Scott tag teamed one of the guys who turned out to be a shapeshifter, morphing into his opponents, trying to confuse them. The third guy, who didn't seem to have any particular abilities, was allowing Byron to take his frustrations out on him until his skin turned into steel. The goth chick's tattoos of barbed wire, a medieval flail, and spiked chains were her weapons of choice besides her fists. They extended outward from her skin and attacked Cheyenne and me. She was quick, but we were quicker and stronger than she was.

We were doing well until I was yanked off my feet and sent soaring across the room. I slammed upside down into the sidewall, landing face down on the floor. Hard.

It was Ronin, who lifted me up by my throat, choking me with one hand. I squirmed and wiggled, but his hold was too strong. He could easily snap my neck if he wanted to, but he didn't. I knew there was no way out of his grip unless I calm down. I stopped struggling and got my thoughts together.

I focused on his mind, imagining it splitting open, but as I did, it backfired on me. Oddly, it still affected him because his knees buckled, let go of me and backed up. I slammed into the floor, gasping for air, but I got up quickly, checking my surroundings, making sure he was still a safe distance away.

He was about ten feet from me, watching me, using the back of his hand to wipe the blood from his nose. He smiled at me as if this was some sort of game to him.

His smile faded as he came toward me, I *credo*, kicked him in the throat and clawed at his eye. Clawing may have been a girly move, but he was scary strong.

He cupped his throat and felt his face but turned around to face me now behind him. I mean, directly at me, as if he could see me.

He stood in front of me before I could move out of the way. He picked me up by my ponytail, tossing me through the air toward the very back wall, away from the others.

I heard a snap when I made contact with the wall. My right leg was broken. Excruciating pain shot throughout my whole body when I struggled to get up.

I wiped away the blood dripping down my face blocking my sight. I held on to the wall, balancing on my left leg while he stood there again waiting for me, toying with me.

Ronin was out for blood, my blood.

I didn't attempt to *credo* again; there wasn't any point in it. My back was against the wall; no one was around us, and I was out of options. He wanted to take his revenge out on me for something I didn't even know anything about. If it were up to him, I was going to die tonight.

"What are you waiting for? Do what you came to do, only don't expect me to plead for my life." I had enough of being afraid, lied to, and stabbed in the back. I wanted this over.

He walked over, stopping so close in front of me; my back was pinned against the wall. "I enjoyed following you around, watching you for the past two years, just waiting. I've watched you sleep like a baby, so many times, wanting to slit your throat, but where is the reward in that? I prefer a good fight then take what I want anyway. Just like your mother tried so many years ago but still failed. Too bad I was too young to be the one to challenge her."

Did he say my mother, as in my biological mother? I had no clue what he meant.

"You have no idea, do you? Why am I not surprised. Those self-righteous *Keepers* are so forthcoming. Your kind leaves the young in the dark for so long, no wonder you are dying off." He laughed, but it sounded more sadistic than anything else.

He gripped the back of my head with his left hand, pulling on my hair as the other cupped my chin. He yanked my head so awkwardly, I had to wrap my hands around his left arm, trying to resist.

But as he stared at me, his grip loosened, his eyes no longer holding vengeance in them. His breathing softened as the shocked expression returned, forcing me to remember who he is to me.

He was everything I knew to be wrong, yet some-thing inside me didn't care.

His right hand started caressing my face, and I closed my eyes, succumbing, allowing him to sway me; it felt so sinfully right. This was mad-ness.

He rested his head against mine and we stayed that way for only a minute. I opened my eyes to look at him. He looked so sad, hurt, betrayed. I didn't understand. I reached up to touch his face and he allowed me to without resistance, but his eyes pleaded with me to stop.

I don't know how, but I knew what he was feel-ing as he was aware of how I felt too. Turmoil. This was wrong, so wrong.

I felt anger stir within him again, and with one brush of his lips across my lashes, he whispered, "I am so sorry." And as he let go of me, I felt emptiness.

This time, his anger was back, ten times worse. I made him feel for the one person he seemed to hate the most. I snapped out of what felt like a trance and came to my senses.

I no longer wanted to care or feel any-thing—not pain, not fear, not even Ronin. So I pushed it away to a dark place in my mind, forgetting it.

He drew out a dagger and drove it at me. I managed to block it, grab it away from him, and toss it. I sliced my hand with it, but I didn't care about the wound, only his next move.

Why wait?

I uppercut him, hitting his nose, and went for his neck, but he blocked my hand and punched me in my face. I hit the ground bouncing but used the momentum to kick him in the gut. When he stumbled back, I jumped up only for him to kick me in my side with his boot. I fell and slid to the wall right next to a huge floor plant. As he came at me, I grabbed a handful of dirt and threw it in his eyes to distract him while I used both feet to kick him in his chest, knocking him back.

I ran up, landed on top of him, pushing his eye sockets to the back of his head, grinding the dirt in them. I started pounding his face in, taking all my frustration out on him. He punched me in the jaw a few times, but I came back until he bucked up, throwing me off him.

I landed on my stomach, scrambling for the dagger, but he was on my back, grabbing for it too. We struggled with the dagger until it broke in half against a statue.

He flipped me over, sat on top of me, pinning my arms down. I stared back at him, breathing hard. "You put up a good fight. You're stronger than you look, but you are out of options. What are you going to do now, Connor?" he said out of breath, purposely letting his blood drip on my face. I turned my head as some landed in my mouth. He smeared it across my lips. It tasted salty sweet.

He was right. I was out of options, so why not piss him off? That was my only card to play, so I played it. "Tell me how ironic it is that the one you were sent to retrieve is the one person you truly feel connected to. Isn't that the real reason you have been following me around all this time? Isn't that the real reason why you hate me so much?"

He said nothing but stared at me. He slowly put his hands around my neck, slowly squeezing, then forcefully so, as if he was working his way up to killing me. He was choking the life out of me. I clawed at his hands, unable to free myself. I moved from side to side, reached for anything, and saw it about five feet away. I waited for an opportunity to free myself, hoping it would not come too late.

My opportunity came with the help of a cry. That was all the time I needed him to get distracted and loosen his grip. It was merely a second but long enough for me to call for the knife that Tony gave me. It had fallen out my pocket earlier in the struggle. I caught it, thrust, and twist it in his neck with all my strength.

He fell backward, grabbing at the knife, feeling shock and hurt, and for a brief moment, I felt guilty, but I pushed that feeling away. I scrambled out from under him and watched him as I braced against the wall. He pulled out the knife, slowly got up, and stumbled toward me.

I expected him to stab me with it, but he didn't. He just stood there watching me as blood oozed down his side, some squirting on me. He was shaking, insanely rotating the knife in his hand, barely able to keep his eyes open.

I flinched as he raised his other hand, placed it in his own blood, and wiped it across my face pulling me close then whispered in my ear. "Sleep tight, for the next time we meet, I may be standing over you."

I knocked his hand back and pushed him away. He kept staring at me as he walked backward, stumbling toward the others.

Tony rushed over to help, but I yelled at him to leave him alone. Tony shot me a puzzled look. I don't know why, but I did. Maybe I wanted him to suffer and die or to give me answers if he lived. Maybe for another reason I cannot admit to.

One of his minions caught hold of him, helping him toward the portal that, in all the commotion, I didn't even notice had opened up.

Right before they reached it, Ronin pulled away from his helper and grabbed Cheyenne by the back of her head. It looked like he whispered something in her ear before taking the knife that was in his hand and plunged it in her stomach. Still holding on to her by her head, Ronin looked back at me, smiled, then let go. And just like that he went through the portal, taking the light with him all before Cheyenne hit the floor.

She didn't see it coming. It all happened so fast that the others could not reach her in time. Cheyenne lay on the floor, choking on her blood.

This is not happening. She can't be dying. I could barely see; my eyes were covered with blood. I was trying to hold it together, thinking why her and not me. He could have killed me.

"Listen, I need you all to keep it together. She is stronger than you think. All of you are. I need you all to gather around now. She is fading fast. You must put one hand on her stomach and touch each other with your other," Tanzia was saying.

"Now close your eyes and concentrate. I need you all to be in sync with each other. Become as one. Once that happens, you can begin to heal her," Tanzia explained.

"Listen to the beat of her heart and slow it down to where all of you have the same heartbeat. Once there, you must picture the wound. It doesn't matter that you see it differently, what matters is the wound you see in your mind is closing. You see it. Now imagine it closing, and at the same time, let your energy flow into her."

We did as she said and became as one. I felt an energy surging between all of us. It was a warm surge of energy that grew stronger and stronger, almost impossible to contain, then like that, it broke.

Cheyenne took a deep breath, then opened up her eyes. We grabbed her up so tightly we almost squeezed the life out of her. Who would have thought I would be happy to hear her make a noise?

Chapter 34

AFTERMATH

Shortly after the dust settled and things were calmer, we took refuge where we could find it. I was on the couch with Cheyenne's head in my lap and was okay with that. It is the least I could do since she almost died twice tonight and lost her best friend.

The guys were laid out on the floor, battered and bruised. Between the three of them, they shared three black eyes, one broken nose, a couple of broken ribs, and a broken arm; and those are just what we figured.

Bynder and Tanzia formed a search party with the *feelers* and others I have never met before to search the mansion for the missing *Keepers* and Mr. Conway, the grandfather. Tochia stayed behind for protection's sake, but she looked more drained than we did. As she lay comatose on the couch, I wondered if it took all she had to attack Tanner. She kept saying she would be fine in a few when we asked. I figured more like a few days.

We were trying to put the missing pieces together when Tochia sat up, holding on to the couch for support, and filled in what we missed, "Willow screamed for help when someone dragged her through the portal, but Mr. Conway walked through voluntarily. Unfortunately, Willow allowed herself to become a victim. She had no clue what she agreed to, but Mr. Conway did. Like his father, he too made deals without telling whole truths."

She further explained that the portal opened up from the other side, bringing an unexpected attack with it. That is why Bynder became otherwise occupied, allowing Ronin to come after me.

"Cheyenne, what did Ronin whisper in your ear?" I asked.

Scott came over to help her sit up. "I don't really remember. It happened so fast, it's hazy. I vaguely remember him saying something about being a shifter. I don't remember. The only thing that stands out is a burning sensation in my stomach, then blackness," she said.

"That doesn't make any sense. If he wanted to kill anyone, it would have been Connor. He all but told us so earlier...," Byron said.

"Wait, Byron, what did he say to you again, Cheyenne, exactly?" Tochia got up and walked closer to us. She sat on the coffee table, holding her right arm that was swollen and bruised.

Cheyenne was trying to recall what he said by mouthing it silently to herself at first. "I don't remember. It all happened so fast," she said, shaking her head. "Do you think it's important, or was it just to get one of us and I so happened to be there?"

Tochia just stared at her, then me, got up, and walked away. Cheyenne and I looked at each other, then asked in unison, "What!"

She was so deep in thought, I asked her a question to get her attention. "Does this have something to do with my mother?" I asked.

Finally, she walked back over to us and sat back down on the coffee table. Taking a deep breath, she explained, "Ronin's intent was not to kill Connor but to retrieve her so I don't know what went wrong. Trust me if he wanted her dead she would be. I have always felt we should tell you both sooner but was outvoted for numerous reasons." Tony came and sat next to me on the armrest, and Byron sat down next to Tochia on the coffee table.

"Now I can only tell you what we have heard second— and thirdhand. It was said that, Connor, your mother..." She held up her hand, stood up, and turned around toward the balcony where Tanzia so happened to be standing. "I know, Tanzia, but they should know... Yes, I know what we agreed... Good, they are all right."

"I have a right to know. I had someone who attacked me tonight, and I didn't have a clue why. Who is he really?" I all but yelled at Tanzia. If they won't give me answers then I don't feel obliged to tell them everything, especially what happened between Ronin and I. How do I explain something to them or Tony when I don't even understand it myself.

Tanzia never responded; she looked at me for a minute until something behind us caught her attention. Selene and Shak came up from the direction of the basement, followed by Bynder and a few of the *feelers*.

"Sorry, Byron, weareunabletolocateyour-grandfather," Bynder said to Byron who put his head down and said nothing. Tony went over to him, but he said he was all right.

We made room for them on the couch. They explained how they were blindsided by a shape-shifter and Khan. He must have dazed them be-cause after that, it was black.

"You all were right, he betrayed us," Selene said. "Technically in the end, Selene, you were saved by

Khan. Tanner did not know where you were. That was obvious when I asked about you two. So it stands to reason he had to have saved you both," Bynder explained.

"Tanner," Selene said, sounding angry. "We should have known. I am disappointed in Wil-low. All she had to do was come to one of us. We would have told her not to trust an outsider and to give him blood vials.

"Who switched the vials?" asked Tony. "I get Khan may have intercepted ours, but not yours. Why even help us in the end?"

"I switched all the vials. I have suspected him for a while. I discussed my fears with Tanzia only after she came to me with hers. I had him followed by *feelers* who confirmed what I had suspected. He disappeared too often for a man who is nothing less than reliable at worst, and when nunans appeared sooner than normal, I knew my fears were confirmed. I was not aware of Willow's involvement, but I'm sure it was minimal," Bynder explained.

"Yes, that is why when he first dropped the vial, nothing happened, but figured if I go into a trance, they would not hazard a clue," Tochia said.

"So it's normal for us to do that?" I asked. "Go rigid and stiff."

"Yes, it is a defense mechanism for protection's sake. Khan has always expressed to us he's wanted more than this lifestyle, but I never expected this from him. I hope he finds whatever he is looking for on the other side and never come back because if he does, I will be waiting for him," Shak said.

"I want to go after Willow and my dad," Byron said

"I say we don't. I'm not risking my life for traitors," Scott said.

"Even under the best of circumstances and if you were well trained, you would not survive. Besides, they are most likely already dead unless they can find a use for them. Willow is the only one worth any value, and by the time you get to her, she won't be the same person," Bynder said.

"How cruel can you be?" Cheyenne asked.

"He is being honest. Bynder knows firsthand. He is lucky to have walked away with just that scar," Tanzia said.

"I'm sorry, but I don't care. She was tricked. Believe me, she had no idea what she got herself into. I'm going with or without any of your help. I will find a way." Byron made it clear that no was not an option.

We had barely banned together, and we had already fallen apart. Byron's grandfather was missing, Willow, Mr. Conway, and Khan betrayed us, and Byron wanted to go on a suicide mission after them. Are they even alive?

Then there is Ronin. What is so important about me? What did he say to Cheyenne, and why stab her and not me? There were so many secrets and unanswered questions, like why did Bynder go to Ether and what really happened to my biological mother? Should I go with Byron to Ether to get some real answers? There's only one thing I knew for sure: today was not the last time I will ever see Ronin.

Dear reader,

We hope you enjoyed reading *The Keepers*. Please take a moment to leave a review, even if it's a short one. Your opinion is important to us.

Discover more books by Dormaine G at https://www.nextchapter.pub/authors/dormaine-g

Want to know when one of our books is free or discounted? Join the newsletter at http://eepurl.com/bqqB3H

Best regards,

Dormaine G and the Next Chapter Team

The story continues in:

The Revealed

To read the first chapter for free, please head to:
https://www.nextchapter.pub/books/the-revealed

The Keepers
ISBN: 978-4-86747-527-0 (Large Print)

Published by
Next Chapter
1-60-20 Minami-Otsuka
170-0005 Toshima-Ku, Tokyo
+818035793528
28th May 2021

Lightning Source UK Ltd.
Milton Keynes UK
UKHW041837140621
385519UK00001B/150